TERRY'S
APPOINTMENT
AND OTHER SPANKING TALES

First Edition

Christopher Trevor

TERRY'S APPOINTMENT

AND OTHER SPANKING TALES

First Edition

Published by The Nazca Plains Corporation
Las Vegas, Nevada
2007

ISBN: 978-1-934625-08-8

Published by

The Nazca Plains Corporation ®
4640 Paradise Rd, Suite 141
Las Vegas NV 89109-8000

PUBLISHER'S NOTE
Terry's Appointment and Other Spanking Tales is a work of
fiction created wholly by *Christopher Trevor's* imagination. All
characters are fictional and any resemblance to any persons
living or deceased is purely by accident. No portion of this book
reflects any real person or events.

Model, Leo
Cover Photo, Corwin
Art Director, Blake Stephens

Acknowledgements

For Pat - You are the ultimate submissive...

For Master Jeff - You are a true spanking Master

For Bill - For years of friendship and for understanding my twisted nature...

For Leonnard Sir!!! - In service to you!!

TERRY'S
APPOINTMENT
AND OTHER SPANKING TALES

Christopher Trevor

CONTENTS

SPANKING INTRODUCTION

In my first book "The Executive Guide to Foot Fetishism and Office Discipline" there appeared a story entitled "The Junior Executive Learns a Lesson the Hard Way." In that story a handsome and muscular junior bank executive named Michael Warner unwittingly finds himself being reprimanded for a banking error by having his Vice President spank his butt cheeks in his private office after working hours…and after all the other office staff has gone home for the day. This story put to rest and threw out the window the theory that an adult male is too "old" to be given a spanking as a means of discipline. Spanking is the oldest form of discipline in the world…and too many people think that just because a man is of adult age he will not benefit from a good old fashioned ass thrashing. The way of spanking a man, the instruments that can be used vary from person to person that administers the punishment. My personal favorite is a round leather paddle. Within five hard swats to an upturned bottom the message has already been gotten across to the recipient. Five to ten hard swats with a leather paddle is usually enough to have the strongest and staunchest of men sniveling, so please do not be stingy with your swipes when swatting a man's butt cheeks with a leather paddle. Each swat and swipe speaks volumes to that guy who is presently over your knee. If he is truly paying attention he will get the message that what he is being punished for is not to be repeated. Other instruments for spanking that some choose are an old fashioned wooden spoon, a leather belt, a wooden fraternity paddle that the spanking recipient has from his college fraternity days and some simply choose to use the back of their hand when disciplining and tanning a man's behind. Wooden hairbrushes are also a personal favorite for some when it comes to this form of teaching. When I set out to put together a book of stories that center around spanking a guy

I sent four questions out to some of my buddies who are disciplinarians and some who are bad boys in need of a spanking and some hard-core discipline. The questions were:

Why do you think it benefits an adult male to be spanked by another guy?

Is an adult male too old to be spanked?

Why would an adult male seek a spanking mentor?

What reactions do you feel, besides a stinging ass when you are spanked?

The replies I received were pretty in-depth and some were very straight to the point...

For my good buddy Joe it is erotic *and* emotional: His physical and emotional attractions are to MEN. Joe enjoys making a man feel vulnerable yet protected by him. Those elements are key as far as Joe is concerned. To be stripped naked (or perhaps down to his underwear as many disciplinarians seem to favor) by another man and to stand before that man who is fully dressed is the ultimate humiliation and feeling of vulnerability, yet it is safe because the stripped man knows that in the arena he is presently in and that he has submitted to his vulnerability will be protected. Spanking is symbolic for caring. "I need to teach you something because I care about you." Upon completion of the spanking there is the connection that I will not leave you, I care about you.

Master Jeff, my best spanking buddy says that most men he has spanked claim that it is a good release for them of pent-up pressures and aggressions. In the lead story for this book we see where that is put to truth in "Terry's Appointment."

Dave, who lives in Florida and has been both spanker and spanked replied by saying that spanking is "GOOD" discipline and training for an adult male. It reminds that adult male that he is "NOT" always in charge and that he is "NEVER" too old for this form of discipline. As for why an adult male would seek a spanking mentor Dave says, "In some ways an adult seeks out a spanking mentor to capture the essence of his youth again. Smiling almost sheepishly when he replied to the question of how he feels when he is spanked Dave said that he feels humility and humiliation depending on his mindset. Also, a sense of submission comes over him and even a feeling of being loved and getting some much needed attention.

Then there are the control issues that my friend Ron the boss man pointed out...

Ron says: "There aren't many chances on a day to day basis for a man to give up total control to another man. Giving up one's ass to a good spanking by another man is an excellent example of giving up total control. The submissive gets the chance to really and truly let go, to surrender in full to another man, as a form of bonding. The dominant in this case has the benefit of taking control of another man, which is a very powerful emotion. Like Joe and Dave, Ron believes that a man is NEVER too old to be spanked. As for why an adult male would seek a spanking mentor the boss man believes that the submissive is looking for someone to take the reigns so to speak. The man who is to be spanked is tired of being in control every minute of everyday, if that is what his life and work entails. He wants a situation where someone else is controlling him for a change, training him, disciplining him, just as he trains and disciplines perhaps people that work for him or the way he disciplines his children when needed.

Nick Bowman, a fellow writer offered this when I put my questions to him:

Assuming that we're talking about a punishment level spanking here, the main benefit is that it makes clear that the adult male is responsible for his actions and attitude. It also addresses free-floating feelings of guilt or inadequacy. And don't overlook the endorphin rush. No adult male is too old to be spanked. If you look at penal codes, nowhere do any say that older people get lesser punishments. While age may be a mitigating circumstance- diminished responsibility is the legal term, if I remember correctly- it is not a "get out of jail free" card. Nick Bowman says that he knows a spanking top who particularly likes punishing men 50 and older because he just knows that they've been doing something wrong- especially if they wear proper business suits. Some adult males miss the direction and discipline they received as boys. Others like the feeling of someone watching over them. I feel an incredible sense of shame and humiliation- what I call the small space. I also feel relieved, as if a weight were lifted off me.

Lastly, my poetic buddy and dreamer Adam says that a spanking is to teach a guy a lesson if he gets out of line "AND" to let him know that there is more where that came from...if required...

TERRY'S APPOINTMENT

Authors note: This is a fictional story; however, it is a story of true bonding between two men. It shows complete trust, compassion and a certain brutality all at the same time. Terry Dean Bradshaw is every disciplinarian's dream...He is a man consumed with rising in the corporate world, yet unaware of his own inhibitions and shortcomings that hold him back from achieving his truest potential. He is a topnotch executive, yet he lacks that push, that drive so desperately needed to propel him to the position of Vice President in the corporation where he is employed, a position he desperately craves, for various reasons other than for himself. It is at the center of his core the reason that this man's man covets such a high position in the corporate world... Enter Disciplinarian and stickler for rules Master Jeff and Terry Dean Bradshaw learns the errors of his ways...the hard way...so to speak. Master Jeff takes the no-nonsense topnotch executive under his wing (and places him under other devices as well) and with a hardhearted commitment from Terry Dean Bradshaw; Master Jeff becomes the executive's mentor, confidant and strictest of authoritarians. Terry Dean Bradshaw shows his nobility and stature as a man's man by standing by his commitment to Master Jeff, realizing that once a deal is made "there is no turning back."

Author's further note: The listing of questions that "Master Jeff" puts to Terry Dean Bradshaw on the night of their meeting I lifted directly from a questionnaire that "Master Jeff" himself was kind enough to give me. It is a listing of questions that all men should think about and reply to at some point in their lives... It is the listing of questions that brings Terry Dean Bradshaw and Master Jeff together in their truest of bonds...

The Story:

Terry Dean Bradshaw, homeowner, staunch corporate executive, a man on his way up the professional ladder with no intention whatsoever of stopping at just Vice President, family man, a guy who has it all, and some secrets as well, one in particular that *only* his good buddy, a man he calls "Master Jeff" can be of assistance for where a certain *need* is concerned. Terry Dean Bradshaw, five feet ten inches tall, he has wavy salt and pepper colored hair cut and styled neatly in a classic banker's style, matching neatly trimmed thick mustache, gleaming blue eyes that could seduce just about any woman, or man if you should so prefer... Terry Dean Bradshaw, ruggedly handsome and a senior corporate executive with a top of the line brokerage firm in New York City, the financial capital of the world. Terry Dean Bradshaw, a man's man in his early forties, well-toned and muscular and in well-developed shape from his daily workouts at the health club four nights a week after work and once on the weekends. Terry Dean Bradshaw, praying to be promoted to Vice President, a promotion he believes is long overdue in coming... Terry Dean Bradshaw, happily married for better than twenty years at this point in time, he and his beautiful wife Wendy have two children, a son, Terry Junior and a daughter, Amanda... Terry Dean Bradshaw, deep voiced, is a Brooks Brother's suits, Hermes shirts and ties and Gold Toe socks wearing gentleman. As pointed out he is a man's man. A man's man who on this Friday night after work arrives at "Master Jeff's" home in the Greenwich Village area of Manhattan. He goes to "Master Jeff's" home every other Friday night for his expected "appointment", his "sessions" as they are called as well...his sessions in discipline and self control, along with the ability to contemplate well under pressure without showing what he is thinking and feeling. The handsome executive lives with the fear that "Master Jeff" will increase his sessions to every Friday rather than every other. Terry Dean Bradshaw's wife and children think that he has a meeting with his superior manager every other Friday and in a way he does...*he really does...*

"Good evening Master Jeff Sir," Terry said, his voice deep and rugged sounding, yet with a nervous twinge to it as well as he walked into his good buddy's home that Friday night, clad spiffily and sharply in a navy blue pinstriped three thousand dollar Brooks Brothers suit.

"You are three minutes late Terrance and promptness is a valued trait," Master Jeff said in stern response, closing and locking the door after admitting his guest into his home. "What do you have to say for yourself, anything? Anything at all?"

Terry knew that he was three minutes late, but inwardly had hoped that Master Jeff would have either not noticed or would have let it slide this time, no such luck though. The man that Terry called "Master Jeff" was militant when it came to the rules of punctuality. Actually, when it came to "the rules" Master Jeff was militant with everything. Any rule broken even slightly could cost Terry and he knew it, *God almighty but he knew it.*

"I'm sorry Master Jeff Sir, the train delayed and then I got stuck waiting for a light to change as I crossed the street," Terry explained as Master Jeff rolled his eyes in his head in disbelief that he had to listen to the executive's boring excuses. "I didn't want to walk out into traffic and risk being hit by a car Master Jeff Sir…and you and I both know Master Jeff Sir that I can't use a company car to get to our meetings, too much would have to be explained and…"

"Yeah, yeah, yeah, excuses, excuses, blah, blah, blah, and yadda, yadda, yadda," Master Jeff said, sounding irritable as he walked toward the bar in his living room, Terry following slowly behind him, almost like a shamed puppy, his big meaty hands crossed behind his back. "You want a drink before we get started tonight Terrance?"

"Only if you're having one Master Jeff Sir," Terry replied, standing in the center of the living room at that point, watching Master Jeff as he poured half a glass of red wine for himself.

It was Master Jeff's favorite drink, red wine, a nice soothing merlot that he favored, always had, *always*, since that night when Terry had met the man he called Master Jeff. Terry stood practically at soldierly attention with his hands crossed behind his back…sweating, the armpits of his dress shirt damp with his manly perspirations. He knew well to stand in that position, seeing as Master Jeff insisted upon it. Terry's cock also began to stand at attention in his suit trousers. Truth be told, Terry's cock had started to stiffen in a mixture of fear and ecstasy since he had left his office to head to Master Jeff's home.

"Well, I am having one, but I just decided that you're not after all," Master Jeff said, held up his glass, mock toasted his guest, said "Bottoms up Terrance", laughed meanly and sipped his wine. "Consider it punishment for your tardiness. A corporate executive such as you should know better when it comes to promptness."

"Yes Master Jeff Sir," Terry replied, sounding totally humbled. "You are correct as always. And just to reiterate I am very sorry for my tardiness Master Jeff Sir."

"Okay, no time like the present to get started," Master Jeff then said, putting his wine down on the bar. "Got to get you disciplined and then back home to the little wife and kids after all…"

Terry looked apprehensively over at the coffee table where all of Master Jeff's "equipment" was neatly laid out and lined up. The executive stifled a gulp of fear and quickly turned his gaze back to the man he called "Master Jeff."

"Well, you know Master Jeff Sir, I was sort of thinking about our session all day today and even on my way over here on the train and…" Terry began, sounding nervous as all hell.

"You were thinking?" Master Jeff asked the handsome and striking executive, sounding totally mocking as he took a sip of his wine. "I do suppose that there's a first time for everything then huh Terrance?"

"Well yes, yes, I suppose there is Master Jeff Sir," Terry replied as he was ridiculed, his hands crossed behind him starting to feel as sweaty as his underarms. "But, as I said Master Jeff Sir, I *was* thinking how I really did do very well these last couple of weeks, since our last session that is. I was kinder to staff members at work, I treated my vice president with the utmost of respect and I even treated a good buddy of mine to an expensive cigar."

"And your point is?" Master Jeff asked and took another sip of his wine, staring steely eyed and impatiently across at Terry as he stood there looking handsomely regal in his suit and tie.

"Well Master Jeff Sir, I was thinking, and my point is this, being that I've behaved exceptionally well these last couple of weeks, I was thinking that perhaps we could skip tonight's session, you know, postpone it till the next time…"

Master Jeff's eyes rolled in his head, a look of total disbelief filling his face…

"Again Terrance?" Master Jeff snapped. "Again we have to go through this prattle of yours?"

"Well Sir, I mean, *Master Jeff Sir, oh God, Master Jeff Sir,*" Terry said beseechingly, already knowing that his request had fallen on deaf ears. "I just thought that maybe…*maybe…*"

"You are not here to think, are you Terrance?" Master Jeff asked in reply and Terry slowly nodded "no." "Don't you even remember the rules that you, YOU, agreed to or do you need a refresher course in listening? We each have a role here that we both firmly agreed to. At this moment I am adhering to my role. You, my numb nutted executive are not! I am really starting to be surprised on how you made it up the corporate ladder so far. You stop thinking right after you leave that fancy office of yours. Do you remember the last time you asked me to postpone a session?"

By now Master Jeff sounded totally angry.

"Y-yes Master Jeff Sir, I remember," Terry said through trembling lips.

"What did I do in response to that request you so called high and mighty executive?" Master Jeff asked.

"Y-you gave me, I mean, oh God, I did it again, Master Jeff Sir, you administered to me forty extras just for asking a stupid question and..." Terry babbled.

"Exaaaaaactly," Master Jeff said, making it sound like Terry was the dumbest corporate executive to ever grace God's green earth. "Now, it seems that lately every time you come here I have to listen to how good you've been, how wonderful you've been, how fucking thoughtful you've been..."

"Well, no, Master Jeff Sir, not every time," Terry said as Master Jeff put his wine glass down, held up a hand halting Terry's talk and stepped over to his handsome charge.

"Now, lets get this straight shall we Terrance?" Master Jeff asked, twining his fingers around the top part of Terry's expensive silk necktie, right under the well done Windsor knot. "You are not here to try to convince me to postpone sessions. You are here for your sessions. You are not here to tell me how wonderful you've been to people you work with or people who work for you or to your wife or even to your kids. That stuff is no matter to me. What matters to me is that you are here for sessions. I am here for sessions. That is what *we* are here for Terrance. You and I are here for our agreed upon sessions. Sessions Terrance, sessions, *sessions*..."You got all that so far?"

"Y-yes Master Jeff Sir, so far I've got it," Terry replied as Master Jeff tugged on his tie a bit and held up his other hand again, silencing Terry's talk again.

"Good, I'm glad to hear that we're on the same page at this point," Master Jeff said sarcastically. "You are simply here to do as I tell you, *that*, and nothing more! Is *that* clear??"

The threatening tone of Master Jeff's voice sent a chill of expectancy, (of ecstasy?) as well as fear directly up Terry Dean Bradshaw's spine. He felt himself starting to twitch uncontrollably with the knowledge of what would soon be in store for him.

"Yes Sir, Master Jeff Sir, it's clear," Terry said, sounding totally defeated yet he repeated the memorized litany that the man he called Master Jeff had taught him…painfully. "Master Jeff sir, I am here because I agreed to accept you in full as my disciplinarian and to assist in relieving me of two weeks worth of built-up stress from my corporate job. I am here because I agreed to hand myself over to you for these sessions, knowing how much you truly care about me Sir. I am here Master Jeff Sir because you are a true disciplinarian and I am in much need of the services you render upon me."

"Good, now unlike last time for making such a stupid request I'm not going to give you forty extras," Master Jeff said and Terry looked somewhat relieved for a second. "I'm going to give you fifty extras."

The look of relief that had been on Terry's handsome face a second ago quickly evaporated. He balled his big hands behind him into a huge fist of apprehension. He could actually feel his ass cheeks tingle at the thought of fifty extras…

"And besides fifty extras perhaps you should spend some time in the corner," Master Jeff said, sneering like an angry parent at his handsome executive. "Because of your repeated tardiness and your apparent mindless questions and excuses *you will* stand in the corner. You will stand at military attention, in just your socks and underpants, with your eyes blindfolded for fifteen minutes of reflective thinking, totally without movement."

Terry swallowed hard…he came to realize that Master Jeff was going to be extra severe with him during the upcoming session. And in a way it was his fault and his alone. What had he been thinking asking Master Jeff to postpone a session? Yet as fearful as he was feeling a very deep and secret part of him was feeling overjoyed at this turn of events. His cock tingled in his suit trousers. Tonight Terry would be able to give up control totally and let Master Jeff do all the work…as it were and so speak.

"Now, climb out of this corporate uniform of yours and down to the uniform you wear for me," Master Jeff said, letting go of Terry's tie.

"Y-yes Sir Master Jeff Sir," Terry said, reaching with his shaking hands and fingers to start undoing the knot in his tie first.

"And you know the rules Terrance, tell me what happens once that fancy tie is off you," Master Jeff commanded.

"Master Jeff Sir, once my tie is off me there is no turning back, once my tie is off me you own my ass and every other part of me until you decree otherwise," Terry said, repeating what he said each time Master Jeff had him in his home, repeating the words that he knew so well by now, slowly undoing his tie as he said his mantra, looking like a man who has made up his mind about his present situation. "If I decide to leave now I am free to go Master Jeff Sir, but, once I slide this tie off my shirt collar the rules are all yours."

Master Jeff nodded with total satisfaction and finished off his wine as Terry got his tie off... As Terry put his tie down on a nearby living room chair Master Jeff prided himself on how well he had trained the handsome corporate executive. He watched lustfully as his charge shucked off his suit jacket, hung it neatly on the back of a chair and began unbuttoning his crisp white dress shirt, his big hands and fingers seeming to tremble as he did so. The wedding band on Terry's ring finger of his left hand was a mocking symbol of part of who the man was. As he undid his expensive gold cufflinks and got his shirt off Master Jeff took in the sight of the executive's robust chest under his white tee shirt. The way Terry's plump nipples pressed against his tee shirt was beyond erotic in the sadistic yet loving master's eyes. Terry laid his shirt on the chair and quickly shucked his tee shirt off, revealing a hairy, muscular barrel like chest and huge, well proportioned massive pecs, two of the plumpest pinkish brown nipples and a flat washboard stomach region. Terry's shoulders were nearly as wide as a doorway; his arms were long, sinewy and muscular, adorned with biceps the size of two bowling balls. His hands, when fisted were big enough to punch holes through walls with, yet his long well proportioned fingers showed the inward sensitivity of a piano player, a writer, or perhaps where Terry Dean Bradshaw was concerned, a painter. Master Jeff could tell that besides the discipline he endured at his hands the handsome executive punished himself extensively at the gym as well. Master Jeff wondered how many times a night Terry Dean Bradshaw's wife wanted him. He wondered just how much sleep the beyond handsome executive actually ever got. As the ruggedly good looking executive bent down to unlace his highly shined lace-up black wingtip shoes his luscious melon shaped ass cheeks outlined beautifully and erotically in his suit trousers. It was those ass cheeks that were Master Jeff's pride and joy. It was those ass cheeks, shaped like two round hard melons that Master Jeff had (secretly?) fallen totally in love with. It was those ass cheeks that Master Jeff loved so much, loved to torture most of all with all, not some, *all* of his implements. And Terry Dean Bradshaw was his truest dream made flesh. The man had proven time and again just how much he could endure being disciplined (tortured?) with ALL of Master Jeff's implements. The man was a staunch executive in every respect of the word. Terry got his shoes off his feet, placed them neatly under the chair where he'd piled up his clothes and then stood up straight, unbuttoning his suit trousers as he did so. The look of fear and apprehension on his face was incomparable. He was such a willing submissive and Master Jeff had to thank God for having brought Terry to him, although he would never let Terry Dean Bradshaw know that, at least not during one of their sessions. In his heart Master Jeff truly loved this man and if he couldn't have Terry Dean Bradshaw as a permanent lover then he would settle for the every other week sessions that they both played their parts for. Master Jeff had come to realize how both he and the handsome corporate executive played their parts very well indeed. Master Jeff chuckled as he thought of the times when he had threatened to increase Terry's sessions back to every week rather than every other week. Terry slid his suit trousers down and stepped out of them, folded them neatly, placed them on the chair with the rest of his clothing and then stood almost at attention before Master Jeff in just his Brooks Brothers burgundy silk boxer shorts and OTC (over the calf) Gold Toe brand navy blue nylon dress socks.

"Now you're in uniform for me," Master Jeff chuckled, noting how Terry's cock was hard as a rock, the tip of it just about peeking out of the fly opening of his boxer shorts, his big juicy balls outlined just inches lower in the boxers.

"Y-yes Sir Master Jeff Sir," Terry said, quickly placing his hands behind his back and standing up even straighter, jutting his massive chest outwards.

"How does it feel being stripped of your corporate uniform, your power suit as you call it, and standing there in just your damned underpants and socks?" Master Jeff asked Terry.

"Master Jeff Sir, it feels humiliating, totally humiliating," Terry replied, his gruff voice belying his underwear and sock clad appearance.

Besides his cock being hard and beefy in his silk boxer shorts Master Jeff took note of the fact that Terry's bulbous nipples had become erect and hard. They were the size of two pencil erasers on the executive's massive chest. It seemed to Master Jeff that whenever Terry stood before him in this manner he was always plumped up big and hard in his executive style silk boxer shorts and his nipples followed suit as well... Master Jeff marveled at how Terry Dean Bradshaw had been blessed with two such oversized and luscious looking nipples. The way they pointed out from his hairy chest was erotic in every sense of the word. This was the uniform that Master Jeff decreed his charge should wear, because nothing humiliated a man more than to be seen in just his underpants and dress socks.

Terry Dean Bradshaw, a man very used to giving orders all day to staff and colleagues, a man very much used to being totally in charge in his domestic home, now stripped of his pride and manhood as he stood before the man he called "Master." Yes, Terry Dean Bradshaw was a man VERY, very used to giving orders on a daily basis both in his professional and domestic lives. He was also a man used to having his orders followed to the T. But here, in Master Jeff's universe all of that power the man imbued went out the window. In Master Jeff's world Terry Dean Bradshaw was able to relinquish all control one hundred percent. For the time he spent with Master Jeff the feeling of relinquishing control was both headily wonderful and awfully painful, an erotically delightful mixture to the corporate executive. Being a corporate executive carried with it a lot of responsibility and power. Wearing what Terry Dean Bradshaw called his "power suit" emanated that power to his underlings. Never did he remove his suit jacket at work like his office underlings. He felt that his complete suit was his armor, but now, stripped to his silk boxer shorts and socks he felt that shield of armor was gone. He had literally been stripped of his power (suit). Truthfully he had stripped himself down to his boxer shorts and socks but at his master's orders it was as if Master Jeff himself had stripped the executive down. When Terry and Jeff (at the time they met that was how they addressed each other, the title of "Master" for Jeff came when they had decided on their first session together) had discovered a while back how this kind of relationship could serve both their secret needs a friendship so trusting, a friendship like no other was born for both men. With a look of trepidation on his face Terry again took in the sight of the equipment on Master Jeff's coffee table. Lined up neatly and ready for use was a round leather paddle, (Master Jeff always began the sessions with that damned paddle) a wooden rectangular shaped paddle with small holes drilled into it (a fraternity paddle Master Jeff called it, a superb device to remind the executive of his college days while in his fraternity active's clutches), a hairbrush, an old fashioned large wooden spoon, a leather strop, and last, but certainly not least an old belt that had once belonged to Terry's step-father, a man who at one time instilled fear, loathing, raw lust and a strange hunger at the same time in the man who was now a corporate ladder climber. When Terry had reached his early twenties he had moved out of his mother's and step father's house. He lived in the dorm of his college campus (another place where he continued to endure having his ass reddened it seemed). His stepfather hadn't seemed to notice that the prized belt that he used to whip Terry's ass with a few times a week when the young man's mother was not around had gone as absent as his handsome stepson. Terry had taken the belt with him and kept it as a reminder of the man who had come into his and his mother's lives and had somehow mastered him. Terry kept that belt close at hand to remind himself of what he had suffered at the hands of his wicked stepfather, to remind himself that no one, no one would ever have him in such a fashion again. But as time went on and the dreams haunted him it seemed that Terry Dean Bradshaw realized that there was a secret and very deep part of him that craved and hungered for the discipline his stepfather used to mete out on him. Even though he was paddled by the actives when he pledged the college fraternity he did not see that as discipline. That was part of being able to endure so that he could become a member of the elite fraternity. It was also a college-boy ritual that he somehow looked forward to. Discipline would come again years later. It wasn't until Terry and Jeff met on a fateful night when Terry's secret needs would be fulfilled once again and he would give his newfound master his stepfather's belt as a symbol of his devotion. Master Jeff decreed how being worked over with an instrument that had been yours and your stepfathers before you made the experience that much more intense and that much more humiliating. Terry was inclined to agree as he recalled how when he was a teenage jock his stepfather reddened his ass for him at least twice a week, sometimes more than twice a week with that very belt. Terry, standing there scantily clad also recalled how his step dad had always, for whatever the fuck the reason made Terry leave his socks on for his ass whippings. Sometimes he was allowed to leave his underpants on, most times they were off, to really get at his meaty jock ass as his step dad used to call it, but his socks, always he was left clad in just his damned socks. (Terry always recalled his stepfather seething as he spanked him with that belt and saying things like, "Yeah boy, nothing teaches a lesson better than having your meaty jock ass reddened like a tomato huh? Fucking meaty jock ass you got here boy! Bet you inherited this meaty ass of yours from your Dad huh? 'Cause sure as shit rolls downhill your mom doesn't have a meaty ass like yours Boy!") As the memories played havoc with Terry's mind he glanced down at his navy blue dress socked feet and nervously wiggled his toes. When he was a teenaged jock it was predominantly white sweat socks that he wore, but now, as an adult, as an executive it was these dress style stinkers he wore. Being stripped down at his stepfather's orders and then having the man whip his ass with that belt made Terry feel worse than violated yet sleazily aroused somehow at the same time. He came to believe that the arousal had more to do with his strength in being able to take what his step-dad dished out on him. When it came to his sexuality Terry Dean Bradshaw prided himself on being a real ladies man. But his stepfather whipping his ass... It was a memory and a need that would follow him for his entire life it would seem. Amazing to him though how his stepfather in the past and Master Jeff now in the present made him strip down to his underpants and socks for his sessions.

"Okay, now that you've stripped down and bared yourself to your uniform of humiliation and humbleness for me go and find your corner," Master Jeff said sternly. "You'll spend fifteen minutes standing at attention in your corner and reflecting and then we shall proceed as we usually do."

"Yes Sir Master Jeff Sir," Terry said, hunched his broad shoulders out and padded on socked feet across the room to a corner of his choice.

Choosing the corner he would stand in like a child was one luxury Master Jeff allowed his charge...

Terry stood in front of the corner of his choice, faced it, took a deep breath, stepped as far into the crack of the wall as possible and with his cock now totally erect in his silk boxer shorts he balanced himself at a stance of soldierly attention...

"Good boy," Master Jeff said from across the room, once more taking in the sight of Terry's delectably shaped ass globes as they filled out the back of his under shorts.

Master Jeff adored how this rugged, masculine man had so trustingly handed himself over to him where his "secret" needs were concerned, his needs also being a desire for "stress relief." Making the corporate executive stand in a corner like a misbehaved child was very humiliating, granted, but that is why Master Jeff insisted on it where his handsome charge was concerned. Stripped to his underpants and socks and humiliated Terry was, yet at the same time fully and wholly erect, his cock straining in the confines of his silk boxer shorts as he obeyed his master's commands. It is always the given Master Jeff thought, how the excitement of the challenge that the topnotch guy had accepted could cause that, as well as his latent submissive nature. Terry knew what he was in for each time he reported to Master Jeff at his home. Being treated in such a way at these "disciplinary" sessions was a reminder for the executive of his carelessness in the past that would stop him from achieving his personal best, his true potential.

As Terry stood with his nose pressed against the corner and as his cock turned to concrete in his underpants the corporate executive found that in this moment of his ordered time of reflection he recalled the night when he and the man he had come to call "Master" first met. Funny, Terry thought now, how when he first met Master Jeff he would not have in a million years thought about addressing him by that title. Now, he could think of no other way to address the man who'd had such a profound effect on his life. To help his charge to reflect and meditate properly Master Jeff stepped behind Terry and tied a soft white cloth blindfold over the executive's eyes.

"Thank you Master Jeff Sir," Terry said, even though in truth he hated being sight-hindered.

Master Jeff gave Terry's backside an openhanded swat and then poured himself a second glass of wine...

"Fifteen minutes Terrance," Master Jeff said softly.

Terry nodded and in his mind saw the bar a few blocks away from the Wall Street office where the company he worked for was located. It was a Friday night, six PM and it had been what most executives would call "A week from hell." Terry Dean Bradshaw, an up and coming vice president could think of no better way to end the hectic week than with a couple of what he called "stiff ones." Clad very sharply and spiffily in a charcoal colored Armani suit, a crisp white custom made shirt, a black silk necktie and a pair of Kenneth Cole highly shined black loafers

Terry Dean Bradshaw sauntered into the Wall Street bar, aptly named "The Wall Street Local" in honor of the fact that it was frequented by the locals of Wall Street, or to be more appropriate, the "Bulls" of Wall Street. The place was dimly lit and decorated tastefully and elegantly ala Wall Street. Small round tables adorned one side of the bar where after-work business could be discussed if the executive patrons desired it. A pool table dominated a second room where young "Wall Street" bulls challenged each other and gambled away thousands of dollars on a game or two, their suit jackets off, their shirt sleeves rolled up and their ties pulled down as they engaged in some intense games of Pool. The front of the establishment was where the main bar was, where Terry Dean Bradshaw was headed for his after work "stiff ones." Terry made a commanding appearance as he sauntered up to the bar, carrying his attaché case. He placed his attaché case on the floor under the straight-backed barstool where he always sat when frequenting the bar, it was his usual spot.

"Good evening Mr. Bradshaw," the middle aged bartender said as he placed a square napkin on the bar, in front of where Terry would be sitting.

"Good evening Craig," Terry said as he shucked off his suit jacket and draped it on the back of the barstool.

As he did so he said "Good evening" to the gentleman who was seated next to his usual spot at the bar. The man was about five feet eight inches tall, he had short cut brown hair and brown eyes and was wearing what Terry would call "Harold Lloyd" spectacles. He appeared to be of average build and was clad in a brown suit, a white shirt opened at the neck with no tie and brown slip-on loafers. Terry guessed the newcomers age to be in the mid forties or thereabouts. The topnotch executive did not (yet) know this man but he had said "Good evening" to him anyway, he was a proper exec after all.

"Good evening to you too," the gentleman said to Terry as he sat down and hefted his feet onto the rung of his barstool.

The man raised his glass to Terry and took a sip of what appeared to be red wine.

"The usual Mr. Bradshaw?" Craig the bartender asked Terry as the man sitting next to him said, "I'm Jeff" and held out a hand, in Terry's opinion, a very big and meaty sized hand, a hand that seemed over-sized for the man's height and build.

"Uh, good to meet you Jeff, I'm Terry, Terry Dean Bradshaw,"

Terry said and shook hands, Jeff's big hand gripping his good and tight.

"Interesting name," Jeff said as he pumped the executive's hand real hard, taking in the sight of his gold cufflinks with some kind of a company logo etched into them, a definite proclamation to his stature at whatever he did and wherever it was he worked, also the monogrammed custom made white dress shirt.

"Thanks, I'm uh, named after my dad," Terry said and as Jeff held tight to his hand he turned to the bartender.

"I'll have a..." Terry began and without thinking why he glanced at Jeff's glass of red wine on the bar.

"It's red wine, merlot," Jeff said and finally let go of Terry's hand.

"Yes, red wine sounds good Craig," Terry said to the bartender.

"Coming up Sir," Craig said and turned to fetch the executive his drink.

Terry fleetingly wondered why he ordered red wine in place of the usual scotch on the rocks that he usually had. It was obvious to Terry that Craig had been totally prepared to serve him his "usual."

"You seem to be pretty well known here," Jeff said and sipped his wine, facing forward as he spoke. "The bartender greeting you by your name and you by his, pretty impressive."

"Pretty well known I would say, I come here fairly regularly," Terry replied, looking at the man as he spoke. "I know this sounds a lot like a cliché but I don't recall ever seeing you in here Jeff."

"That's because it's my first time here Terry," Jeff said. "I'm meeting a client. What is Terry short for?"

"Uh, Terrance," Terry replied. "I like being called Terry though."

"Fine, I'll call you Terrance," Jeff said, sounding almost sarcastic as the bartender placed the glass of red wine in front of Terry.

"Um, okay, sure," Terry said and picked up his glass of wine. "To new friendships Jeff..."

"To new friendships Terrance," Jeff said and clinked his glass against Terry's.

"Yes, to new friendships," Terry replied, thinking, "I suppose..."

"So, what sort of client are you waiting for?" Terry asked after taking a long and satisfying sip of his wine. "What business are you in?"

"I'm a behavior modification therapist," Jeff said. "I specialize in

28

stress control…"

"Ha, bingo!" Terry said and leaned back on his barstool. "You win the prize Jeff…"

"I am guessing you are a stressed out executive," Jeff said, turning and facing Terry, a stern expression on his face. "And a family man no doubt…"

"Bingo again Sir," Terry responded, not knowing at that moment that he would eventually be addressing Jeff as "Sir" on a regular basis.

"What do you do?" Jeff asked raw lust and some sort of primal desire filling him as he took in the sight of the regally handsome man seated beside him.

"I work as a corporate executive for a brokerage firm here on Wall Street," Terry replied and sipped his wine. "I'm in charge of two departments, lots of money involved, and its pretty heady stuff all day."

"I bet it is," Jeff said.

"So uh, what kind of therapy do you use for your clients?" Terry asked. "Maybe I'll come to your office sometime for a session or two…"

"I require a commitment of more than just *a session or two* Terrance," Jeff said, sipped his wine and knew that he had just hooked another frontrunner.

"Well, I suppose that would be okay, seeing as I'm always stressed out after a long hard day at work," Terry said, seeming to be surmising his timeframe.

As Terry sipped his wine Jeff noticed the wedding band on his ring finger. The man had a wife. He was right when he'd said that he was a family man. That always made it more intense and more interesting, both for him and for his charge. In Master Jeff's opinion there was nothing more intensely intriguing than having a married man, some woman's husband under his control.

"Okay, let's say I make a commitment of five sessions," Terry began and chugged down what was left of his wine.

As he set his glass down Jeff raised a finger at the bartender and almost instantly two more glasses of red wine were set down, one in front of Jeff and one in front of Terry.

"I require a commitment of at least ten sessions to start with Terrance," Jeff said, reaching into his pocket and producing a business card. "The kind of therapy I treat my clients with is seriously intense, very hard-core and to some *very* terrifying, yet, if you are a person of substance and inner strength it can be the most rewarding of experiences you ever submit to."

"Wow, now you really have my curiosity piqued Sir," Terry said, turned on his barstool facing Jeff and lay one foot over his knee. "I consider myself to be very strong both mentally and physically. With what I do for a living I better be strong, sharp and focused. But at the end of the day the stress just seems to crawl all over me...and..."

"...and that's where I would come in..." Jeff said and handed Terry his business card.

Terry looked at the card (seen below) and his chin dropped as he stared at it, his other hand pausing as he was raising his glass of wine to his lips.

MARK SOL
555-555-1234

"What in hell is this?" Terry asked, holding the card between his thumb and first two fingers of one hand as he sipped his wine.

"That is my business card Terrance," Jeff replied sternly. "The kind of therapy I mete out is not the Freudian or Jung or new age methods. I don't use religion or any of that mumbo jumbo to treat my clients with. I dish out strong discipline. I demand total obedience and from that you will learn true self control. I am a strong believer in the healing powers of serious "spankology."

Terrance, still looking at the card, glanced up at Jeff and looked back at the card again. His hand seemed to be trembling all of a sudden as thoughts of his stepfather filled his mind.

"S-spankology?" Terry asked, almost in a whisper. "Y-you mean you spank your clients?"

Jeff simply nodded "yes" slowly and sipped his wine.

"And *that* relieves them of stress?" Terry asked. "Being spanked relieves them of stress???"

"Yes, as it would you Terrance," Jeff replied. "It would relieve you of stress, cause you to learn self control, AND, and, at the same time I would force you to stretch your limits."

"Spank me? Spank me???" Terry asked, sounding shocked at the fact that Jeff had even suggested such a thing, yet for a fleeting moment seeing his stepfather's face in his mind. "Man, you have got to be kidding! The last person that ever spanked, paddled and whipped my poor ass was my step dad when I was a teenager! Okay, when I pledged a fraternity in college I was paddled but that was different, that was all college hi-jinks!"

"So what you're saying is that at this age a therapeutic spanking would not benefit you," Jeff said, staring forward. "In my opinion it would benefit you greatly Terrance."

"How, how so?" Terry asked.

"Terrance, if we are going to continue this conversation I will insist on something right here and right now," Jeff said, looking into his glass of wine as he spoke.

"What's that?" Terry asked.

"You begin addressing me as "Sir"," Jeff said sternly. "Being the disciplinarian I am it's only proper that I should be addressed as such. I'm sure you're properly addressed by your underlings where you work."

Terry looked at Jeff in disbelief, pursed his lips tightly for a moment and huffed, but for some reason heard himself saying, "Okay, Sir it is, if you insist on it, Sir."

"Insist I do," Jeff said.

"But I'm not your underling, Sir," Terry said and took a gulp of his wine, not believing that he was actually having this conversation.

"Not yet you're not," Jeff chuckled and Terry winced for a moment.

"Okay Sir, now, if you would be so kind as to answer my question," Terry continued, still looking at the card in disbelief that he had been handed. "How would *you* spanking *me* relieve stress and force me to stretch my limits? What limits are we talking about here, Sir?"

"Well, have you ever felt that you have not reached your fullest potential in certain areas of your life Terrance?" Jeff asked.

"Uh, yes, in way I feel like that sometimes, Sir," Terry replied.

"How so?" Master Jeff asked.

"Well, I feel that where I work I should be a vice president at this point, Sir," Terry replied. "And with the way I work so hard I think I am being shafted."

"My form of therapy would help you to realize the error in that line of thinking and I would force you to see how it's you and your own ineptitudes that are holding you back from achieving that much coveted title in your workplace Terrance."

"M-my ineptitudes? Now hold on there Jeff, Sir," Terry said through clenched teeth. "I am not inept…at all…"

"Then why aren't you a vice president where you work?" Jeff asked and sipped his wine. "Since we started talking here why have you been so defensive?"

Terry simply looked at the man as he sipped his wine, took a deep breath and whispered the words, "oh shit." Jeff, facing forward, set his wine glass down and nodded "yes."

"Ten sessions Terrance, *to start with*," Jeff said and as he said it Terry felt that he should bolt from the bar, to get away from this strange man he had just met, instead he sat as if fastened to his seat.

"To start with Sir?" Terry asked sounding totally nervous yet he could not believe that his manhood was stiffening in his suit trousers.

His curiosity was more than piqued at that point…

"Yes, it appears to me that you are a very highly competitive, stressed out, high socked executive who is in dire need of regular sessions with me," Jeff said. "I specialize in only highly competitive people who can thrive on discipline and control…to be able to relinquish their control to me for the duration of spanking sessions."

"High socked," Terry chuckled. "I like that for some reason Sir. Uh, if that's your professional opinion…"

"It is…" Jeff replied quickly, cutting off Terry's words while at the same time praying that this beguilingly handsome man would submit to him.

The thought of having this rugged and masculine married man under his control was the headiest of feelings he had had in a long time. He could tell from the look on Terry's face that the man was terrified yet intrigued at the same time.

"Ten sessions to start with, once a week," Jeff said. "Then after that I will have you report to me every other week on an agreed upon day and time. When you agree to that day and time you will adhere to it religiously. Part of training you will be to teach you the value of being prompt and always, ALWAYS on time for your appointments."

Terry nodded, not believing that he was actually agreeing to all this. *Was* he agreeing to all this? He squeezed his black socked ankle as it rested on his knee and realized that *yes, he was* agreeing to this. Somewhere deep inside him he knew this need resided…and Jeff seemed to be the man to serve that need for him.

"Okay then, once a week Sir," Terry said, gulped his wine and found he was fighting tears as they filled his beautiful eyes. "What uh, what day are we looking at, Sir?"

"Terrance, now that you've agreed the rules will become even more rigid," Jeff said. "From this moment onward you will address me as "Master Jeff Sir…" Is that clear and understandable to you?"

"Y-yes, I suppose so," Terry said, his lips trembling and he quickly finished his wine. "Master Jeff Sir…"

"Very good Terrance, very good," Master Jeff said.

To Terry it at first sounded totally ridiculous, but somehow, as he said it, looking at the man he had just addressed as Master, he felt a stirring deep down in his loins. He had not felt like this since the days of his stepfather… Obviously, the high-powered executive realized, there was still some deep seeded need within him for discipline.

"Master Jeff Sir," Terry said again. "What day would I be required to meet you for…uh, to report to you for sessions?"

"Does Friday nights work for you Terrance?" Master Jeff asked and reached forward to take Terry's left wrist in hand, eyeing his wedding band. "Did you call your wife tonight to tell her you would be home late, seeing as you're here in "The Wall Street Local" bar?"

"I, uh, no, Master Jeff Sir," Terry replied. "She uh, she can't know about this, ever..."

"That Terrance, is not my problem nor did I question that, I simply asked if you had called her to tell her you would be home late," Master Jeff said, holding Terry's wrist tight, taking in the sight of his cufflinks, his wedding band and the Rolex watch under his shirt sleeve.

"The only time I call her to tell her that I'll be late is when I get stuck working on special projects or if the computer system where I work goes down Master Jeff Sir," Terry said shakily. "Those are things that would keep me at work longer than usual Sir. She works part time for a jewelry company and Friday nights are usually her late nights. If not she'll just get home and think I'm still at work. I would think that Friday nights would be satisfactory then Master Jeff Sir. I could tell her that going forward I'll be working late for about one..."

Master Jeff held up two fingers on his other hand as he caressed Terry's sleeved wrist with his other hand.

"Two...two hours every Friday night for the next ten weeks Master Jeff Sir," Terry said, his tears filling his eyes to nearly overflowing at that point. "And then every other week after that."

"Good man," Master Jeff said and his heart thundered in his chest at the sight of the crystalline-like tears that had flooded his new charge's eyes. "I assure you Terrance, this is the best decision you will have ever made for yourself... You see my executive, discipline derives from *disciple*-disciple to perhaps a philosopher, disciple to a set of principles, disciple to a set of values, disciple to an overriding purpose, to a super ordinate goal or in this case, me, a person who represents that goal."

"Yes Master Jeff Sir, if you say so," Terry said and snuffed back his tears.

"Well, shall we be on our way to my place then?" Master Jeff asked. "I don't live too far from here."

"N-now Master Jeff Sir?" Terry asked. "But I thought you said you were waiting for a client."

"I was, you're here now," Master Jeff said and let go of Terry's wrist. "I'll meet you outside. Pay for the drinks and order a car for us. I live on Fourth Street and Avenue B. Also, be sure to call your wife and let her know that you'll be late in getting home tonight...and for the next nine Friday's as well."

"Y-yes Sir, Master Jeff Sir," Terry said and sprang to his feet.

He stood there paying the tab, watching out of the corner of his eye as the man who he would from that moment on call "Master" strode out of the bar with a confident swagger in his step. As Terry waited for his change from the bartender he again looked at Master Jeff's business card. He gulped hard…wondering what in the Sam hell he had agreed to here tonight…yet somehow he could not (did not want to?) turn back; inwardly he knew that as well as he knew his own name…

A short while later Terry stepped out of the bar called "The Wall Street Local" and stood beside Master Jeff.

"Did you do as I instructed you Terrance?" Master Jeff asked as Terry stood, shifting his attaché case around in his hand.

"Yes Master Jeff Sir, I did as you instructed," Terry replied. "I paid the bar tab, I used my cell phone to call my wife to let her know that I would be late tonight and a cab is on the way Sir."

Master Jeff nodded, looked at Terry and said, "Very good, very good so far Terrance. Perhaps as it is your first night in session I'll just hold onto you for an hour and a half rather than the allotted two hours."

"That uh, that is up to you Master Jeff Sir, it is not for me to decide," Terry said and then a fancy service car pulled up in front of the two men…

Before the driver could get out and open the door for Terry and Master Jeff Terry did the honors of opening the car door for his newfound friend, mentor and master…

"Yep, you do learn fast Terrance, I will give you that," Master Jeff said as he stepped into the car and settled into the plush seat.

"Okay, lets begin the usual way," Master Jeff said now, jarring the blindfolded Terry back to the present as the executive stood in the corner, reflecting on the past.

Stepping over to his stripped down handsome charge Master Jeff hooked a hand around one of the man's upper arms, his hand of course not making it all the way around Terry's huge bicep. "Let me tell you what you're in for this time you numb nuts executive. Let me show you just how stupid you were to hand yourself over to me tonight."

"Y-yes Sir Master Jeff Sir," Terry said, the feeling of Master Jeff holding tight to his arm almost claw-like.

"I'm going to begin by giving you the fifty extra swats you earned by asking me a stupid question," Master Jeff said in an explanatory sounding manner. "That will be a reminder to you as an executive to never, NEVER ask stupid questions, whether it's here or in your world of work. Those swats I will administer to your hairy ass cheeks with my leather paddle, twenty-five consecutive swats to each cheek. After that warm-up I'll give you ten swats with the leather paddle again, those for your tardiness. Five swats to each ass cheek this time. Once those hot ass cheeks of yours are warmed up and primed the way I like them we'll get down to the regular business for your session. Any questions so far you numb nuts executive?"

"N-no Sir Master Jeff Sir, no questions," his eyes filled with tears behind his blindfold and his lips trembling as he tried to speak clearly.

It had only been a short fifteen minutes that he had stood in the corner but the tension was showing. Terry's muscular body was perspiring more than ever from the feeling of dread mixed with anticipation. Master Jeff took his charge's blindfold off him and still held tight to Terry's arm.

"Okay Terrance, time to go to the spanking couch and get this show on the road what do you say?" Master Jeff asked Terry.

"I, it's not mine to say Master Jeff Sir, it's yours to say and yours only," Terry said softly as he walked on his socked feet beside Master Jeff to the spanking couch.

Master Jeff sat down and pointed at the leather paddle...

Without a word of resistance or complaint Terry picked up the leather paddle, kissed it twice, once on each side and handed it to Master Jeff. The regal looking corporate executive then got himself situated over Master Jeff's lap and knees, his socked toes pressed hard against the floor as he balanced himself in the most humiliating of positions. He folded his arms and pulled them up behind him. He was glad for small favors as Master Jeff didn't tie him this time... But the session hadn't actually begun so he could still wind up tied the ruggedly handsome executive thought somewhat miserably...

"Okay Numb nuts, count off the swats for me," Master Jeff said, rubbing the leather paddle against Terry's silk boxer shorts covered ass cheeks. "For the warm-up rounds I'll leave your fancy shmancy silky boxers on you. After we're done though you're going through the regular session bare assed."

"Y-yes Master Jeff Sir," Terry said, his head hanging down, looking at the floor as he spoke.

Inwardly it amazed Master Jeff that this strong minded and very take charge corporate executive could put himself in such a mortifying and degrading position. But the boner that Terry was sporting in his boxer shorts as it pressed against Master Jeff's lap told him that Terry was right where he was meant to be at that moment. Master Jeff had to wonder what the executive's wife would think seeing her man this way. It seemed that many, many Wall Street corporate executives craved this kind of treatment at the end of a long and hectic week. Giving orders and being in positions of command eventually took their toll and it was good therapy to let go and allow someone else to take charge once in a while. Master Jeff was pleased that Terry had found him…and he planned to have "sessions" with the handsome executive for as long as time would allow.

"And you'd better count correctly you numb nuts," Master Jeff said with total authority in his voice, moving the leather paddle over Terry's hairy and muscular thighs and upwards over his melon shaped ass cheeks. "Tell me what will happen if you miss a number or stupidly repeat a number…"

"Master Jeff Sir, if I mess up on the count we will start back at number one," Terry stated, repeating still more of the rules that he had been taught during his times with Master Jeff.

"Very true story," Master Jeff said, loving the way Terry's ass cheeks looked so beautifully and delectably outlined in his silk boxer shorts.

Master Jeff raised his leather paddle and brought it down hard on Terry's left ass cheek… It made a sound like WHAPPP.

"OWWWWW!!!" Terry hollered. "ONE!!!"

WHAPPP WHAPPP WHAPPP WHAPPP WHAPPP

"ARRRRRHHHHH, and two, three, four, five, six!!" Terry called out loudly, his hands holding tight to his folded arms behind him as he lay across Master Jeff's lap.

"You know Terrance, ten to twenty swats with one of these leather paddles is enough to have the boldest of men sniveling like when they were children," Master Jeff said sarcastically.

WHAPP WHAPP WHAPP WHAPP WHAPP WHAPP WHAPP

"OWWWWWWWW!!!" Terry cried out through clenched teeth. "S-seven, eight, nine, ten, eleven, twelve, thirteen…G-GAWD!!!!"

"But I don't plan on being stingy with you like that, "Master Jeff said meanly. "In your case I'm being really generous here and giving you fifty good hard ones!"

"Y-yes Sir Master Jeff Sir, thank you Sir!!" Terry bantered.

As Master Jeff swatted Terry's left ass cheek over and over and over and over again the corporate executive counted diligently as his cheek seemed to be heating up and stinging more and more with each blow. He kept the count true, gritted his teeth, and held his folded arms tight. For the moment he choked back tears as the blows from Master Jeff's paddle pummeled his ass cheek...but soon enough the superlative executive knew he would be sniveling and crying like a little kid.

"OWWWWWRRRR!!!" Terry ranted and screamed out the numbers. "Twenty, twenty one, OWWWWWWWWWRRR my poor ass globe Master Jeff Sir, twenty two and twenty three!!"

When Master Jeff administered the twenty-fifth and final swat to Terry's left ass cheek Terry screamed out the number twenty five like he was filled with joy, glad that that part of his punishment was over. Master Jeff wasted no time however in getting down to the business of swatting Terry's right sided ass cheek.

WHAPP WHAPP WHAPP WHAPP WHAPP WHAPP WHAPP

"OHHHHHHHHRRRRR oh fuck," Terry cried out, wondering on one hand why he had ever agreed to all this, while on the other hand overjoyed as the man he called "Master" doled out the discipline. "One, two, three, four, five, six, seven!!!"

When Master Jeff completed the twenty five swats to Terry's right ass cheek he congratulated his charge on having counted so well, saying it sarcastically however. Both of Terry's ass cheeks felt like they were crimson, more than likely already matching the color of his silk boxer shorts.

"Th-thank you Master Jeff Sir," Terry gasped, trying desperately not to reach down and rub his stinging ass cheeks. He knew that if he moved his hands from the position they were in Master Jeff would waste no time in tying them tightly behind him... It had happened so many times in the past. Terry wanted so much to obey his master's orders and keep his hands clasped tightly behind him, but reaching down and rubbing one's wounded ass cheeks after being spanked good and red was a natural response Terry had found over time. But Master Jeff would simply tie him if he did so. And Terry had to admit that he hated being tied. (Maybe not?)

"Okay, those were for your stupidity, now for your tardiness,"

Master Jeff said and brought the paddle down good and hard on Terry's left ass cheek, beginning there again.

WHAPP WHAPP WHAPP WHAPP WHAPP

"OWWWWWWCCCHHH!!! One, two, three, four, five!!!" Terry called out.

"Will you be tardy for our next session you numb nut executive?" Master Jeff asked Terry.

"N-no Master Jeff Sir, no way Sir!!" Terry cried out loudly. "It won't happen again Master Jeff Sir!!"

"I didn't think so," Master Jeff chuckled and brought his paddle down hard five times on Terry's right sided ass cheek.

Terry called out the numbers from one to five correctly and wondered if his ass cheeks now matched his silk boxers. He recalled when his wife had bought him the burgundy silk boxer shorts for his last birthday and she said how very sexy he looked in them when they had gone to bed that night. If his wife could see him now in his sexy boxers she would not believe it Terry thought, unaware that Master Jeff had just thought the same thing just a few minutes ago... Actually, for whatever the reason, Terry thought at that moment how his wife purchased all his socks and underwear for him, just like most married guys out there it seemed...

"Okay Numb Nuts, that was a good warm-up," Master Jeff said.

"I-I agree Master Jeff Sir," Terry said, sounding stupid.

As Terry lay across Master Jeff's lap, squirming slightly, he felt the paddle being rubbed over his reddened wounded ass cheeks, and he knew that the warm-up was nothing compared to what Master Jeff would have him endure as the session progressed...

A few moments later, per Master Jeff's orders Terry was standing next to the spanking couch with his hands crossed up behind his head. He had only suffered a total of thirty five swats to each ass cheek so far but being that Master Jeff was expert when it came to the art of spanking the corporate executive was already feeling the burning sting and searing sensations. Master Jeff having ordered him to cross his hands up behind his head insured that he would not reach down to rub his wounded ass cheeks. (Plus, having had Terry cross his hands up behind his head really forced the stripped down executive to show off his beautiful musculature. In Master Jeff's opinion Terry Dean Bradshaw had one of the best bodies he had ever seen. Every inch of the man was solid muscle, barely an ounce of fat on him anywhere.) Master Jeff wanted Terry to thoroughly enjoy and benefit from every moment of the searing hot pain. Plus it was after being well-spanked that the searing sting set in a little more with each passing moment, Master Jeff called this the baking part of one's ass cheeks. Roasting those cheeks came as the session progressed. Terry then watched as Master Jeff placed his leather paddle back down on the coffee table and then picked up the wooden fraternity paddle with the holes drilled into it... Terry nervously wiggled his toes in his navy blue socks, recalling how in his college days those kinds of paddles had been used on him when he was a fraternity pledge and then in turn he used those kinds of paddles on pledges when he became an active. During Hell Week he was paddled at least two to three times a day and he made sure to do the same to his pledges when his turn as an active was finally at hand. He recalled having endured being spanked and paddled in college when he was what was called a "frat pledge" but now he would be enduring it from a true spanking master, not some college boy wanna be master.

"Now Terrance, walk to the spanking table," Master Jeff said commandingly. "And bring your arms down, but be sure to keep them positioned at your sides."

"Yes Sir Master Jeff Sir," Terry said and slowly brought his arms down.

Once Terry was standing beside the spanking table Master Jeff slowly slid down Terry's silk boxers to his ankles, resting his hands on the executive's flaming ass cheeks with a light pinch to induce more anticipation. Terry stepped out of his boxers and tossed them over to the chair with the rest of his discarded business attire. Terry's hard cock pointed straight out, rigid and thick veined, his plump cum filled balls hung down real low, low hangers his wife sometimes called them when she would play lick and slurp with them. Master Jeff made no mention of Terry's erection; he simply stepped behind his charge with the wooden fraternity paddle in his hand and followed Terry toward the huge dining room table of his home... As he walked wearing just his navy blue OTC socks Terry had to admit to a feeling of total and complete humiliation and degradation engulfing him. His cock strummed harder in front of him as he thought of his underlings at work and how they would feel if they saw their manager in this position. His red ass cheeks stung and he knew they would be on fire before the evening was over...

The elegant dining room was dominated by a large oak table in the dead center of the room...

Terry did not need to be told what to do as he stood at the end of the table, awaiting Master Jeff's orders... The table, where in the past numerous dinner parties had been held, had been completely cleared for the spanking occasion... Master Jeff had one time in the past allowed Terry and two of his subordinates to use his home as a meeting place, seeing as their conference room at the bank was booked for the day by other departments. The two underlings enjoyed the fact that they were able to have a meeting in a less business-oriented atmosphere, somehow they were both more productive at that particular meeting, but for Terry it held more meaning than they could ever know. Terry, seated at Master Jeff's dining room/spanking table with his two subordinates, one male and one female and knowing that this was the table where he was spanked sent a chill of elation and dread through him during that meeting...if only they knew he kept on thinking and his cock churned in his suit trousers like crazy at that meeting.

As Terry stood there naked but for his socks he thought how for all the times he was spanked in the past, whether it was his stepfather dishing it out or perhaps an active in college he was always stripped down to his socks. He was always ordered to strip to socks.

"Always spanked in my socks, ALWAYS in my damned socks..." the topnotch executive seethed inwardly as he felt Master Jeff's hands on his red butt cheeks and his mind once more wandered to the past, to that first night when he met Master Jeff at the "Wall Street Local" bar and how he had unexpectedly wound up accompanying Master Jeff home to his luxury apartment. Of all places that he would have thought he could have possibly wound up winding up in that Friday night after work, a spanking master's apartment was the last place he would have thought of...

"Welcome to my home Terrance," Master Jeff said as he guided his blindfolded and well-dressed charge into his apartment.

"Th-thank you Master Jeff Sir," Terry replied sheepishly, holding tight to his attaché case as he was led into the pleasantly scented home.

He detected a scent like lavender in the air and Terry wondered if Master Jeff enjoyed scented candles the way he and his wife did. Master Jeff let go of Terry's arm long enough to lock the door to the apartment. Terry stood docile as he waited to be led further into the place. It was when he and the man he would from then on call "Master" had stepped into the elevator that Master Jeff had said he was going to blindfold him. Terry took a deep breath as his eyes were covered with the soft white cloth and he heard Master Jeff say reassuringly, "Don't be afraid Terrance, this is all part of your training which will begin tonight."

"Y-yes Master Jeff Sir, I mean, no Master Jeff Sir, I won't be afraid," Terry replied.

As he stood there now in Master Jeff's apartment Terry realized that by allowing the man to blindfold him he had shown that he would permit him to take control of him. He had also shown Master Jeff that he trusted him implicitly…and in such a short manner of time at that. Master Jeff took Terry's attaché case from him and set it down in a corner.

"This way Terrance," Master Jeff said, clutching his charge's upper arms in his hands and guiding him into the living room.

Moments later Terry was seated in a straight backed cushioned living room chair, clad in just his blindfold, a pair of plaid silk boxer shorts and his black OTC nylon dress socks. Stripping down out of his suit while blindfolded had proved to be a tad taxing for the corporate executive, but in the end he had managed. His cock was betraying him by plumping up in his silk under shorts, plumping up, and chubbing up, what his wife called it when he became erect in his silk boxer shorts. She claimed that that was part of the reason she purchased them for him. She loved how whenever her handsome hubby wore silk boxer shorts it never failed to cause him to really become erect. She figured it was the feeling of the silk against his thin skinned huge cock that set him in motion where that was concerned. As he sat there blindfolded awaiting his master's orders Terry wiggled his toes nervously in his black dress socks.

"Would you care for a drink Terrance?" Master Jeff asked his newfound "client."

"Only if you are having one Master Jeff Sir," Terry replied.

Master Jeff pursed his lips and an expression of pride came over his face as he stepped to his full wet bar.

"You learn fast Terrance," Master Jeff exclaimed as he poured two glasses of red wine, merlot style.

He handed Terry the glass of wine and told him to sip it slowly. As the blindfolded and stripped executive sipped his wine Master Jeff sat down across from him on the couch, what would be called the "Spanking Couch" in time to come.

"Comfortable for the moment Terry?" Master Jeff asked, facing his charge, taking in the delicious sight of him there in just his underpants and socks and blindfolded.

"Y-yes Sir Master Jeff Sir, I'm comfortable for the moment," Terry replied and carefully sipped his wine.

"The way you were dressed when you came here, in your suit, your tie, your highly shined shoes, that's considered your Wall Street uniform for the day," Master Jeff said. "When you report to me for your sessions you will be clad in the uniform you wear now, just your under shorts and socks. I find that being stripped down the way you are now truly humbles a man. Is that understood so far Terrance?"

"Yes Master Jeff Sir, it's understood," Terry replied and licked his lips.

"When you report to me for your sessions you will always, ALWAYS be on time," Master Jeff went on, sounding stern then. "Any tardiness will not be accepted, nor will any excuses for tardiness be accepted. Promptness is a virtue and one that must be adhered to. Tardiness of any kind will be met with extra swats added to your punishment for that week's session."

Terry nodded and sipped his wine...

"When you arrive here for your sessions you will have time to strip down to your socks and under shorts for me," Master Jeff continued. "Until you take off your tie you are free to leave, in other words you control the situation for the moment when you first arrive here. Once you take your tie off it is a signal to me that you have relinquished control and that I am now fully in charge."

As Master Jeff spoke Terry's cock was by then fully erect in his silk boxer shorts. He could feel it dribbling pre seed and staining the front section of his boxers as he listened intently to his "Master." If Master Jeff noticed the erection that Terry was sporting he made no mention of it.

"I understand Master Jeff Sir," Terry said and sipped his wine.

It was all too much for him Terry thought in disbelief, it could not be him seated there in just his silk boxers and black dress socks, yet it was. All too much to be believed yet he would not get up to leave...not just yet anyway. Fear filled as he was he was also intrigued to the point that he was erect and throbbing in his silk boxers...

"Good, now in order for me as your behavior modification therapist and to assist you in relieving the stress and anxieties you feel I need some information from you Terrance," Master Jeff stated. "For this part of our session tonight you will remain blindfolded for a while. Any time I blindfold you it is to assist you in reflecting on something or perhaps to help you meditate to a state of mind in preparedness for your spanking that night. Do you understand?"

"Yes Master Jeff Sir, I understand totally," Terry replied and gripped one of the arms of the chair he was seated in.

"Good, now tell me, as a manager at the bank you work for how do you treat your subordinates?" Master Jeff asked. "Not how you treat them once in a while, but for the most-part, how do you treat them?"

"Well, Master Jeff Sir, I'm very stern, very uncompromising," Terry said. "But that's only because of the pressure that I'm under from my vice president and..."

"I didn't ask you about the pressure you're under Terrance," Master Jeff interjected, sounding harsh. "Answer the question and only the question..."

"Yes Sir Master Jeff Sir," Terry said sheepishly, thinking of how just recently during that past week he had reprimanded a young female subordinate for making a very small mistake and how she had cried as he reprimanded her in front of the entire office staff.

His cock churned in his silk boxers...

"Do you sometimes belittle the people that work for you Terrance?" Master Jeff asked.

"Y-yes I do Master Jeff Sir," Terry replied and wanted to say how at times it was necessary in order to get things done in a demanding atmosphere but followed orders and answered only the question he had been asked. "I admit that sometimes I treat staff like they were gofers."

Terry found that when Master Jeff asked a question it was best to simply answer the question and not try to add other embellishments to what he said in his reply.

"Do you feel that it's right that you belittle them?" Master Jeff asked.

Terry pursed his lips and grimaced a bit behind his blindfold.

"Terrance?" Master Jeff prodded him.

"I, Master Jeff Sir, I'm not sure how to properly answer that question," Terry said.

"Do you think its right that you treat staff like gofers?" Master Jeff asked.

"Master Jeff Sir, I'm, I'm not sure how to answer that question either,' Terry responded and nervously licked his lips.

"Terrance, the fact that you belittle your staff members and the fact that you treat them like gofers shows me part of the insecurities you have," Master Jeff said. "It is also by belittling them that makes you feel a bit better about yourself, but not by much, it's that insecurity you hide that keeps you from achieving your true potential as a vice president…"

"If you say so Master Jeff Sir," Terry said.

"I say so Terrance, but here, in my private home I will assist you in overcoming those insecurities," Master Jeff said, again sounding reassuring.

"Th-thank you Master Jeff Sir," Terry said and felt tears once more that night filling his eyes, this time behind his blindfold.

Master Jeff stood up, stepped beside Terry's chair and rested a hand gently behind the back of Terry's neck.

"Take off your blindfold Terrance," Master Jeff said.

Terry reached up with one hand and pulled his blindfold off, setting it on the coffee table in front of him. On the coffee table he saw the leather paddle, the fraternity paddle, the hairbrush, the large old fashioned wooden spoon and the leather strop. With his hand trembling he raised his glass to his lips and sipped more wine.

"Those are my tools Terrance," Master Jeff stated as Terry stared straight ahead as his eyes adjusted back to the light and he took in the sight of what Master Jeff had just called his tools. "Each time you come here I will use each of those tools on you, or, to be more precise, on your ass cheeks, and at times when I feel you really need punishment I will also tan the backs of your thighs."

Terry grimaced and gulped hard, feeling like the captured super-hero in one of the comic books he used to read when he was a child. He sipped his wine and enjoyed the warm and mellow feeling it gave him as it slid over his palette down his throat.

"Tell me Terry, when you were young did your father discipline you by spanking you?" Master Jeff asked, his hand still resting gently on the back of Terry's neck.

Master Jeff stroked the executive's soft wavy salt and pepper colored hair. He loved the way it felt so silky against the back of his "bull" sized neck. It was going to be his pleasure to spank this handsome mountain sized muscular executive.

"Uh, yes Master Jeff Sir, but it was my stepfather who spanked me," Terry replied, sounding a tad miserable as he said it. "My uh, my parents divorced when I was a kid and my mom married Glen when I was a teenager."

"And it was Glen who spanked you?" Master Jeff asked.

"Yes Master Jeff Sir," Terry said. "As I mentioned earlier I was actually named for my father, his name having been Terrance that is..."

"Why did Glen spank you?" Master Jeff asked his charge, taking his hand off the back of his neck and sat back down across from him.

"To uh, keep my grades in check, to push me to be a better athlete, to pound respect into me Master Jeff Sir," Terry responded, his eyes filling with tears yet again.

"You hated your stepfather for doing that to you Terry?" Master Jeff inquired, staring intently across at the robust executive.

"I, sometimes Master Jeff Sir, but for the most-part I loved him," Terry said, his tears flowing slightly. "You see, my real dad was not a good provider Sir, whereas Glen my stepfather was. He always took good care of me and my mother. I loved him for that but I hated him for spanking me...he spanked me two times a week, sometimes three."

"How old were you when he did this?" Master Jeff went on.

"Through mostly all of my teen years Master Jeff Sir," Terry replied.

"And you never told your mother?" Master Jeff asked.

Terry nodded "no" and said, "I felt it was something that was just between us men, just as this will be here, just between you and me Master Jeff Sir."

"Terry, look at my tools lined up in front of you," Master Jeff said and Terry did as he was told. "Those are *my* tools, as I've pointed out to you. You will provide me with one more."

"I don't understand Master Jeff Sir," Terry said, but did not look up at Master Jeff as he said it; instead he kept his eyes riveted to where his master had instructed him to.

"Each person I treat with spankology provides me with at least one tool of their own that they will be spanked with," Master Jeff explained. "Usually it's a leather strap that their dad, step-dad, mom, step-mom or guardian used to use on them or perhaps a fraternity paddle that they were made to make while in college and then spanked with by their pledge master. It could also be just an instrument that they bought say in a utensils store, such as a wooden spoon. Some people have memories of childhood and will bring me a wooden paddle that used to have a rubber ball on a string attached to it. I think you get the idea Terrance…Bringing me an object that you were pummeled with in the past will show your devotion to me in what I am administering to you."

"Master Jeff Sir, I'll bring you my stepfather's belt," Terry said. "It's the one he used to use on me."

"You have this belt in your possession Terry?" Master Jeff inquired, his curiosity piqued off the Richter scale at that moment.

"Y-yes Master Jeff Sir, I have it," Terry responded. "When I moved out I took it with me. It's a reminder of what I went through at the hands of my stepfather. It was also a reminder to me that I would never allow somehow to have me that way again."

"Hmm, and here you are after all Terrance," Master Jeff said with a grin.

"Yes Master Jeff Sir, here I am after all," Terry said and gulped down the rest of his wine. "Master Jeff Sir, may I set my empty glass down on the coffee table?"

"You may Terrance," Mater Jeff replied and again felt a sense of pride in how quickly this charge was learning.

Terry placed his empty wine glass on the coffee table alongside Master Jeff's "tools."

"Terrance, before you leave here tonight I plan to spank you," Master Jeff said. "I want you to start getting used to what you will be enduring at these sessions. We will always begin with the leather paddle to redden and warm your ass."

"Yes Master Jeff Sir," Terry replied respectfully but not without a hint of fear in his tone.

"Before we get to that however I'm going to put a series of questions to you," Master Jeff went on. "You'll answer the questions quickly and honestly. Is that clear?"

"Yes Master Jeff Sir, it's clear," Terry said.

"And you do not have to say "Master Jeff Sir" when you reply to each question," Master Jeff stated. "That would take too long seeing as there are a lot of questions. Do you understand Terrance?"

"Yes Master Jeff Sir, I understand," Terry replied and Master Jeff smiled thinly.

*Master Jeff's questions will be written in **Bold** type and Terry's responses will be in regular type.*

Master Jeff reached under the couch he was seated on and produced a sheaf of papers that were stapled together. He began reading the questions that were listed there...

How old are you? I am in my forties.

Where were you brought up? Here in New York City.

Do you feel you are too defensive? Sometimes.

Do you feel that your life is now too stagnant? Yes, even though I am making it in the corporate world I sometimes feel that there is something more that I want.

Do you feel that you need pressure and structure in order to function to your fullest capacity? I really don't like pressure on me at all. Maybe a prod once in a while to get me moving, but no pressure. Structure, yes, I like structure. I like the expected and mostly the routine; although this experience has really thrown a monkey wrench in there I would say.

Would you consider yourself to be unreliable? No, I am very reliable...when I make a commitment I see it through to the end. Just like I'm going to see this through to the end...wherever that end is going to be that is...

Do you feel that you don't think before you act? No, I generally think first.

Do you feel that you get embarrassed much too easily? Oh yes, that is a fear.

Do you feel that you have a hidden "dark side?" Yes, there are times when I have a temper.

Would you consider yourself to be a quitter? No...I will tend to struggle through.

Do you usually look for immediate gratification? Yes, especially when I have done a good job or seen something difficult all the way through.

When you were growing up were you allowed to develop at your own pace? Yes, and no. My stepfather always pushed me to succeed so there was some stress there. My mother was not as pushy, although she was always happy when I did well. She wasn't aware that it was my stepfather was literally beating successful motivation into me, via my ass cheeks.

Do you feel that athletics was "over stressed" in your upbringing? Oh yes, I was heavily involved in athletics when I was a teenager, my stepfather made sure of it and then on my own until nearly thirty. Now the only athletics I engage in is at the gym on a regular basis, if you want to call that athletics that is.

Are you seeking more stability in your life? Yes…sometimes at work I feel very unstable even though I put forth a very stable persona.

Do you feel that you need more realistic goals to follow? No, I just need to focus and pursue the ones I have.

Are you prone to mental or creative blocks where you just can't seem to function? Sometimes, although being the manager I am at the brokerage firm where I work it's hard for me to admit that.

Do you feel that you are a hotbed of tensions, fears and anxieties? No…but at the moment I think I am.

Do you become irritable or annoyed much too easily? Yes…I think it is because I have not made vice president yet at the brokerage firm.

Do you often obsess about death? No, not at all.

Does it really bother you to be alone for long periods of time? I don't like being alone but I am not sure what you mean by long periods of time. I can't say I have ever really been alone for long periods.

Do you often feel that you lack follow through? Sometimes, but not often. Hmm, maybe that's why I haven't been made a vice president yet where I work.

Would you consider yourself to be a sore loser? More of a bad loser not a sore loser…but, if I can lose in the right way it can be exciting.

Do you feel that you are too introverted? I used to be a very shy person but my stepfather managed to beat that out of me as well, again, via my ass cheeks.

Do you often fantasize about violent acts? No.

Do you often feel that you lack common sense? Not at all.

Do you feel that your curiosity often gets you into trouble? It looks like it might have tonight, seeing as I am going to be spanked on a weekly basis from now on.

Do you feel that you are too complacent and laid back? No, I am anything but.

Are you often bothered by feelings of being too self-destructive or self-abusive? Not at all.

Were you often punished for doing poorly in an athletic

event (parent, coach, whomever?) I generally excelled, as I have stated already my stepfather made sure of that. When I did not do well he brought me home and as long as my mother was not there he tanned my rear end for me. Doing fairly well was not tolerated either.

Are you bothered by self doubts almost every time you make a decision? Inwardly yes, I can say that is generally the case.

Do you often feel that you are too incompetent? Maybe just not competent enough, maybe that's another reason why I'm not a vice president yet at the brokerage firm.

Do you feel that academics or achievement was "over stressed" in your upbringing? Oh yes, just read the question about succeeding in athletic events.

Were you <u>ever</u> stalked, or did you <u>ever</u> stalk anyone? There was a girl in high school that seemed to be always after me…but nothing ever came of it. I am not that bold or stupid enough to stalk someone. If they are not interested in me…then I just let them go.

Do you like to seek attention, even if it is negative? No, not negative, although I do like attention brought to me if I have done a good job on a special project at the firm where I work.

Do you feel that self reliance was <u>not</u> stressed enough in your upbringing? No.

Do you often feel paranoid or afraid? Not paranoid but sometimes afraid.

Does it really bother you to be kept waiting? A bit…I can be impatient. That is an area at the firm where I work where that really comes through. When I put an order to an underling I want it carried through as efficiently and as quickly as possible. If it is not I can be a bit unruly to the person who works for me.

Does it really bother you to have others look over your shoulder? Yes, now that is annoying. It makes me lose my concentration.

Do you feel that you "burn out" much too easily? No.

Would you consider yourself to be very moody, with sharp highs and lows in mood swings? No.

Were the arts or creativity stressed enough in your upbringing? No, not really. As it turns out I am a very artsy person, but because of what my stepfather forced me through in my youth I did not have much time for art. I love painting and I love paintings by the masters.

Do you now have a steady girl, lover, or wife? I have a wife.

If so, are you happy with this situation? Yes, she is a good partner. We've been happily married through our better than twenty years together. Other than the usual arguments, stuff about finances, things where the kids are concerned and regular day to day events we're still there for each other. And we've never cheated on each other…at least I never have. I'm sure I can say the same for my wife.

What area of your life do you feel was most stifled in your upbringing? My artistic ability…it was not really stifled, more like just not fostered because I was never really able to express how much I loved art. I spent most of my time at athletics and then over my stepfather's knee.

Do you feel you often try to hide your sensitivity and emotions from others? Yes. I can be very emotional, I will admit to that here and now.

For your age, would you consider yourself to be physically immature? No.

Do you find it really hard to express your emotions? No… not really.

Did you often move while you were growing up? Not at all.

Did you <u>ever</u> seek punishment just for the attention it would put on you? No, not on a conscious level, but it looks as if tonight that subconscious desire has been brought to the surface. I do like seeing a haughty person being punished though.

"Okay Numb nuts, assume the position," Master Jeff said, jarring Terry back to the present for the moment while reaching into his pocket at the same time and bringing out a pair of dice.

"Yes Sir Master Jeff Sir," Terry said and did as he was told.

The handsome corporate executive leaned down over the table, his chest area resting atop it as he did so. He spread his muscular legs as wide as possible and then gripped the sides of the sturdy oak table… Terry's most private crevice, what Master Jeff called to his humiliation his shit chute, his pink valley, his chocolate channel, his anal canal was now on total display along with his low hanging balls dangling between his choice looking muscular thighs. Terry's red hairy butt cheeks were pointing totally upwards and were ready for another good paddling. Chuckling meanly Master Jeff shook up the dice in his hand…

"Recite the rules where the dice are concerned my numb nut executive," Master Jeff said meanly.

"Yes Sir Master Jeff Sir," Terry said. "You will roll the dice and I will receive the amount of swats shown on the dice."

"Hmm, very good so far Terrance," Master Jeff said, sounding again as if Terry was the dumbest man in the world.

"If you should roll double digits Master Jeff Sir, I get double the amount of swats shown on the dice," Terry went on. "As an example, as you always say to give Master Jeff Sir, if you roll double sixes I'll be given twenty-four swats with your paddle rather than twelve."

"Amazing, totally fucking amazing that a numb nuts like you can keep all this straight in that limited mind of yours," Master Jeff said sarcastically.

"I-I do my best Master Jeff Sir," Terry replied, sounding like a little boy trying to please his mother. "Okay, the rules Master Jeff Sir, you will role the dice three times for three sessions, which means I will be walloped for a total of nine rounds.

"You got it Terrance," Master Jeff chuckled and bent down and gave one of Terry's socked feet a squeeze, showing him just a tad of affection.

"And like when you paddled me with the leather paddle Master Jeff Sir, if I fuck up the count we begin back at the beginning..." Terry said, completing his usual prattle where the dice were concerned.

Terry then took a deep breath as Master Jeff stepped behind him at the end of the table and took up position behind his spread legs. Terry knew that even though he was facing away from Master Jeff and would not be able to see the numbers on the dice as they were rolled he knew that Master Jeff would be honest. It was the sure thing the two men knew they both shared, their honesty. They knew from the start of all this that they could trust each other implicitly where certain things within their sessions were concerned, the number on the dice being one of those things. Master Jeff reveled in the mortifying sight of Terry Dean Bradshaw's luscious looking ass and his hole as it stared up at him it seemed, totally on display on his table. The way Terry's muscular legs shimmied down to his sexy huge sized feet, the way his socked toes curled back in anticipation of the upcoming swats, the way the executive's gaping rosebud of an asshole flicked at Master Jeff, the way his sweaty and juicy low hanging balls dangled like Christmas tree balls hung too closely together, all of it spurred the man on the more where spanking his handsome subject was concerned. Terry then heard the sound of the dice being shaken up in Master Jeff's hand. The corporate executive took a deep breath and clenched his teeth as he heard the dice hit the table between his spread legs…

"A five and a one numb nuts," Master Jeff said and aimed his fraternity paddle true against Terry's target of an upturned ass.

WHAPP WHAPPP

"UHHH, one and two Master Jeff Sir," Terry seethed through his clenched teeth.

"Aren't you lucky at the outset of this end of your session?" Master Jeff asked.

WHAPPP WHAPPP

"Yes, yes Master Jeff Sir, very lucky indeed I am," Terry called out. "Three, four…"

WHAP WHAPPP

"And five and six Master Jeff Sir," Terry said, his voice belying the fact that he was already stinging back there."

He heard Master Jeff shaking up the dice for the second set of the first three rounds…

"A five and two numb nuts, seven lucky hard swats coming up for you…" Master Jeff said.

"Y-yes Sir Master Jeff Sir," Terry said loudly and kept his teeth clenched.

WHAPPP WHAPPP WHAPPP

The sound and feeling of the fraternity paddle as it sailed through the air and then connected meanly with Terry's upturned ass was maddening to the first-rate executive.

"One, two, three," Master Jeff Sir," Terry cried out, starting to sweat at this point.

WHAPP WHAPPP WHAPPP WHAPPP

"F-four, five, six and seven…" Terry said glad that the second set of round one was over.

He silently prayed not to have double digits of any kind rolled (or maybe not…) He cringed as he heard the dice being rolled and then they hit the table again…

"Damn, a four and a one you numb nuts," Master Jeff said, rubbing the wooden fraternity paddle over Terry's ass cheeks as he spoke to him, taunting him. "It looks like the dice really love you tonight eh?"

"I-I think it's just dumb luck on my part Master Jeff Sir," Terry replied, his eyes filling with tears of awe as he called out the master's name.

WHAPPP WHAPPP

"One, two, Master Jeff Sir," Terry said.

WHAPP WHAPPP WHAPP

"Th-three, four, and five…" Terry called out triumphantly…

"Good boy so far numb nuts," Master Jeff said meanly and again squeezed one of Terry's socked feet.

Terry knew from past lessons and sessions that the squeezing of his foot meant that he was doing well so far…

"Lets switch to the wooden hairbrush for the next round of dice throwing," Master Jeff said stepping over to the coffee table and putting down the fraternity paddle and picking up the round wooden backed hairbrush. "How do you feel about that numb nuts?"

"Like earlier Master Jeff Sir, what I want or feel is not what matters here, it's all what you want Sir, Master Jeff Sir, and how you see fit to train and discipline me," Terry responded and Master Jeff chuckled, sounding totally sadistic.

"Coming up, round two of dice throwing and spanking," Master Jeff said and shook up the dice, throwing them on the table. "YES, HA!! A six and five numb nuts! Now we're getting to some good numbers huh?"

"Y-yes Master Jeff Sir, good numbers Sir," Terry said despondently at the thought of eleven more swats on his already reddened ass cheeks.

"Good for me but not for you, numb nuts," Master Jeff laughed.

This time he hooked an arm around Terry's mid section and faced away from him, the handsome executive's ass cheeks right in his line of fire.

"And away we go…" Master Jeff laughed and raised his hairbrush, wooden side aimed at Terry's ass.

WHAPPP WHAPPP WHAPPP

"UHHHHH!!! One, two and three, Master Jeff Sir," Terry said and reveled in the feeling as Master Jeff held him tight.

"Sing out you numb nuts executive," Master Jeff chided his charge.

WHAPPP WHAPPP WHAPPP was the awful sound as Master Jeff used the wooden hairbrush to thrash Terry's ass cheeks dead center…right over his gaping and sexy crack…

"Th-three, f-four, five, six…" Terry called out louder but too late realized his fatal error.

"Ah, ah, ah, Terrance, you bad, bad boy," Master Jeff laughed and tightened his grip on Terry's mid section. "You repeated the number three you stupid numb nuts…"

"Oh God Master Jeff Sir," Terry reeled, his head hanging down as he spoke.

"What happens now you bad boy? Tell Master Jeff what happens now…" Master Jeff said, sounding totally fiendish.

"Please Master Jeff Sir, can't I have a break this one time?" the high socked executive pleaded miserably. "I've been so good so far tonight and…"

To cut off Terry's irritating tirade Master Jeff swiped his red ass with the bristles end of the hairbrush.

"AAAYYYYY!!!" Terry screamed. "OH, okay Sir, being that I fucked up the count we will begin this round back at the beginning… Master Jeff Sir…"

"Good boy," Master Jeff said and raised the hairbrush.
WHAPPP WHAPPP WHAPPP

"One, two, three, Master Jeff Sir," Terry counted well and true.

"Good boy lets hear it again," Master Jeff teased his charge.
WHAPPP WHAPPP WHAPPP

"f-four, five and six…" Terry seethed, feeling that each blow was harder than the one before it, causing his stinging ass cheeks to tingle.
WHAPPP WHAPPP WHAPPP WHAPPP WHAPPP

"S-seven, eight, nine, ten and eleven Master Jeff Sir, eleven Sir!!" Terry called out happily.

"Amazing the things that will make a numb nut executive like you happy Terrance," Master Jeff laughed and picked up the dice, giving Terry's low hanging balls a sniff as he reached for the dice.

Terry secretly grinned, despite the pain he was in, as the man he called Master Jeff sniffed his nuts, it showed him that the man really did care for him and all his insults and mean gibberish was all part of the game. But Terry didn't have long to think about all that as he heard the dice shaken up yet again for the second set in the second round… The dice hit the table and Master Jeff announced…"A five and a three you numb nut exec."

"Eight…" Terry said miserably.

"Eight is right," Master Jeff said and again gripped Terry around the mid-section with his arm held him close and raised his hairbrush, wooden side up. "No wonder you're hoping to be up for that promotion where you work…you really can count…"

WHAPPP WHAPPP WHAPPP WHAPPP WHAPPP

"RRRRHHHHHHHH!!!!" Terry wailed as Master Jeff swung harder and harder it seemed with this round of swats to his poor ass cheeks. "ONE, two, three, four, five, Master Jeff Sir…"

"And three more to go," Master Jeff said, his own cock beginning at that point to grow stiff as Terry's delectable looking ass became more and more reddened.

To Master Jeff's eyes Terry's hairy ass was starting to look like an over-sized bowl of red cheery jell-o.

WHAPPP WHAPPP WHAPPP

"Six, seven and eight Master Jeff Sir," Terry called out through clenched teeth. "OHHHHRRRR my poor ass…" Master Jeff chuckled, gave Terry an extra swat with his hairbrush for good luck and laughed meanly before saying, "One more set for this round and then we move on to round three where your poor ass, as you so aptly called it, will get a break…"

"OH MY GAWD, no," Terry sniveled, droplets of moisture forming at the end of his nose as he managed to keep himself balanced on all fours up on the table.

By now the rigidly topnotch and no funny business executive was looking like anything but that…

"You know what I just said means eh Terrance?" Master Jeff asked as he shook the dice in his hands.

"I sure do Master Jeff Sir, I sure as all hell do," Terry said, nearly crying now. "When you say you're going to give my poor ass a break it means that you're going to lash and fire up the backs of my thighs… OOOOOHHHHH GAWD MASTER JEFF SIR!!!"

Master Jeff snickered meanly; Terry would get no compassion at that moment…

It wasn't at every spanking session that Master Jeff would lash and barbecue the backs of Terry's thighs, but when he did it was because Terry was overdue for some deeply needed discipline. Master Jeff also said that it was a good way to once in a while remind Terry Dean Bradshaw, powerful corporate executive just who the hell was in charge where this scene was concerned. In the corporate arena Terry was a man in charge, in the spanking arena Terry was not in charge at all. So while his poor reddened ass was getting a break from being spanked, it really was another torture that the stalwart executive would be enduring. What a double edged sword that was Terry Dean Bradshaw thought miserably.

"Let's get it done Numb nuts," Master Jeff said and threw the dice down on the table between Terry's spread legs and under his very red, cherry jell-o like ass cheeks. "A six and a two…"

"Another eight Master Jeff Sir," Terry said despondently and Master Jeff raised his wooden hairbrush.

After Master Jeff had administered the last eight swats to Terry's now very red ass cheeks with the back of the hairbrush he ordered his charge down off the table and into a new position for the last three sets for round three of the dice deciding number of swats that Terry would receive. With his hands crossed behind his head and his mammoth sized erection saluting Master Jeff, Terry Dean Bradshaw awaited his instructions. If he could just rub his wounded ass cheeks it would mean so much to him he thought…but that was not to be, as Master Jeff wanted him to really feel the burn as it penetrated the skin of his luscious ass globes. It was what Terry needed to help him achieve in his life where he had under-achieved.

The instructions that Terry received were what he had dreaded hearing since coming to Master Jeff's home that night for his spanking and discipline session, Master Jeff was going to tie him, and to make the matter all the worse he was going to tie him to the "Block." With his hands still crossed behind his head, with his huge erection still swinging in front of him like a flagpole, Terry, naked except for his navy blue OTC socks followed Master Jeff most humbly to the sound-proof room. It was the room where the man that Terry called "Master Jeff" kept the "Block." Terry was literally shaking in his socks as he padded behind the man he had totally submitted to for these sessions. Terry's red ass cheeks stung more and more with each passing second, proof that Master Jeff knew just how to administer spankings…

In his hand Master Jeff carried a long leather strop, the next piece of his equipment that would be Terry's instrument of torture. The backs of the executive's thighs stung just thinking about what he was in for now… As they entered the room Terry gulped hard and took in the sight of the "Block" and in what seemed like no time Master Jeff had secured him to it, in one of the most humiliating positions that a man could be secured to a device of this sort…

"Okay Terrance, we'll continue with the dice for the thigh stropping as well," Master Jeff said to his charge.

"Y-yes Master Jeff Sir," Terry said miserably as Master Jeff dashed out of the room to retrieve the set of thrash-deciding dice.

As Terry squirmed sexily and miserably on the "Block" his mind once more wandered to the past, to the night when he and Master Jeff had first met. As he thought of that night his hard cock twitched under him and his cum filled balls churned. He recalled how Master Jeff had made him sit facing him, clad in nothing more than his underpants and black dress socks as he rattled off the questions to him. Terry felt as if he were in a situation between being interrogated and being interviewed somehow. Also, it amazed the superlative executive how at this moment in time, strapped down to the "Block" how he remembered so many of those mind-searching questions...

Do you feel you could use better stress control? Yes. This has been an issue for some time now I would have to say.

For your age would you consider yourself to be sexually inexperienced? No Sir. And I have to say that being spanked will somehow expand my horizons. I just get that feeling.

Do you feel that you are physically weaker than most other males your age? Definitely not Master Jeff Sir, the way I workout keeps me fit and strong.

Were you taught to do what you were told to do without questioning? Yes, but mostly from true authority...not just some asshole that walks up.

Were you taught, or did you experience that a male should not show his feelings, his sensitivity, or his creativeness? Well, not really. That was more of a societal thing that we guys picked up from our peers.

Are you too easily talked into things others want you to do? Yes...I sometimes find that I am rather submissive in that way. It boggles my mind, seeing as I am a strict and very demanding corporate executive...yet there's that submissive side to me as well.

Do you feel that you are compulsively neat and clean? Most times, yes.

What is one of your biggest complaints or gripes about anything? That I have not yet made vice president yet where I work and I work harder than most of the guys there.

Complete this: My life at present is: not what it should be.

I have not achieved what I had pictured for myself to be financially successful. I still struggle financially at times.

Are most of your close friends male or female or about equal? Interestingly, I seem to get on with females better. But my friends are mostly male.

Does that make you think you might do better with a female disciplinarian? Not at all, I think the male bonding thing that will happen between you and I will work for both of our benefits.

Do you feel that you are too easily distracted? Yes.

Do you feel that your life is now too dull or routine? A bit. But after tonight and going forward I doubt that will be the case.

Do you feel you are not as responsible or as mature as most others your age? No.

Were you often complimented while you were growing up? Yes. Not to sound too vain but I was big, very handsome, fairly smart, artistic and as I have pointed out, athletic.

Complete this: I enjoy: I enjoy being with my family.

Complete this: I get nervous when: I get nervous when I have been put on the spot or find myself in a new situation. I also get nervous being made to sit wearing just my underpants and socks.

At that reply Master Jeff chuckled and ordered Terry to stand up and take off his plaid boxer shorts, adding that he had permission to keep his black OTC dress socks on. As Terry stood to do his new master's bidding he blushed sheepishly as his erect cock popped up in front of him, long, thick, beefy and throbbing as his two succulent hairy balls hung down low in his sweaty looking sac. Terry placed his underpants under his chair and sat back down, his legs slightly parted, his balls resting on the chair, his cock standing straight up, oozing pre seed and staring at the ceiling. Master Jeff had all to do to keep his gaze off his charge's most impressive manhood.

Do you feel you could use more discipline and control? If it's dished out by the right person, yes.

Were you ever in therapy? No.

Do you feel that you are under a lot of stress lately? Most definitely.

Would you consider yourself to be the "life of the party"? No, but I am a true participant.

Do you feel that too much was expected of you while you were a teenager? Yes. My stepfather's approach was too hard for someone my age.

Were you considered to be hyperactive while you were growing up? No.

Do you feel that you could benefit from strong behavior modification? Probably from some behavior modification. We will see how the next few weeks go and how I do.

Is it very hard for you to really enjoy life? No.

If you could do or change anything that has ever happened to you in the past, or has ever affected you, what would you do or change? I would have been more truthful about my love of the arts. Instead I put up with being spanked and forced to do things that I really did not want to.

Do you expect too much from others? Yes, I think I do at that.

Would you consider yourself to be a boat rocker? Sometimes.

Do you feel your life is in a constant struggle mode? Yes, more-so now than ever before with the demands of job and family. But please don't get me wrong, I love my family dearly.

Do you usually feel uncomfortable with the opposite sex? No.

Do you feel you are more conservative than most men your age? No, I tend to be libertarian. I would be viewed by most as conservative but I do tend to sometimes have some very different views.

Do you often feel that you are too excessive? Yes, sometimes.

Do you feel that you might be a dysfunctional person? No…not really.

Do you want to be less shy and more outgoing than you are now? Yes.

Do you feel that you have to, or just want to test your pain, endurance or embarrassment levels, even if it means crying or losing face? Until tonight I didn't think so, but now, sitting here in just my socks and ready to be spanked I would have to say yes to that question.

Do you feel that it is important to be accepted or to fit in, even if it means going against your own values? No.

Do you feel that you are prone to unfulfilling relationships? No.

Do you feel that you get upset too easily when things go wrong? Yes.

Who was stricter with you, your mother or father? As I told you, my stepfather.

Do you feel that you have trouble dealing with rage? Yes, sometimes.

Are you often afraid to show affection? No.

Do you feel that you procrastinate too much? No.

Do you often feel that you are too intense? Yes. As I've stated I can be very intense at my place of work.

Do you usually make the first move in establishing personal contacts? Yes, like tonight when I sat down next to you at the bar.

Do you feel you should be more adventurous? I'm about to be.

Is it overly hard for you to keep friends? I don't usually lose friends. The situations change and the relationships seem to become history.

Do you often feel so depressed that it is hard for you to function? No.

No...No...No...that was the word that was racing through Terry Dean Bradshaw's mind now as Master Jeff sauntered back into the soundproof room. In one hand the man that Terry had come to call "Master" held a pair of dice. In the other hand he held the long leather strop that for three rounds would redden the backs of the executive's muscular thighs. Terry squirmed miserably on the "Block" and held his tears in check...for the moment.

"How are you feeling there my numb nuts executive?" Master Jeff asked his charge, the look in his eyes one of absolute fiendishness.

"Apprehensive Master Jeff Sir, I'm feeling very apprehensive," Terry replied and squirmed on the block, his already reddened ass making a pretty picture in his master's eyes.

"Looks to me like this has been a very productive session so far," Master Jeff said and ran the palm of a hand over Terry's red ass cheeks.

Terry flinched a bit at Master Jeff's touch...

"Now, let's get the backs of those thighs reddened shall we?" Master Jeff asked and held up the dice.

"It, it's not for me to say Master Jeff Sir," Terry said, sounding miserable now as he recited his mantra.

Master Jeff chuckled and shook up the dice in his hand. Terry watched from his strapped down vantage point as Master Jeff dropped the shaken dice to the floor...

Terry's eyes nearly popped out of his head when he saw the double sixes staring up at him mockingly while staring up at Master Jeff triumphantly.

"Oh Good Lord," Terry whimpered, sounding totally fearful now.

"Double sixes my executive," Master Jeff said, taking up position beside the terrified Terry. "And you know that when double digits are rolled..."

Master Jeff paused in mid-sentence and pointed at his charge...

"When double digits are rolled I receive double the amount of swats shown on the dice, Master Jeff Sir," Terry recited, finishing Master Jeff's litany for him.

"Very good Terrance," Master Jeff chuckled. "And I'm sure that a first-rate executive such as yourself knows that twelve doubled is..."

Once more Master Jeff pointed at Terry...

"...t-twenty-four Master Jeff Sir..." Terry said shakily. "Tw-twelve doubled is twenty-four!"

"Very good Terrance," Master Jeff said. "Now start counting..." That said Master Jeff swung his arm back and brought the leather strop crashing down on the backs of Terry's thighs.

"AAAYYRRRRR!!! One, Master Jeff Sir!" Terry cried out, sounding almost pitiful.

SWATTT SWATTT SWATTT SWATTT SWATTT SWATTT was the sound as the leather strop landed over and over across the backs of Terry's trapped thighs...

"T-two, three, four, five, six...S-SEVEN!!!" Terry screamed in a high-pitched tone of voice. "Oh God Master Jeff Sir. "Is this really necessary tonight???"

SWATTTT SWATTTT SWATTT SWATTT SWATTT SWATTT

"Eight, nine, ten, eleven, RRRRRRRRRR!!!!" Terry cried, literally. "...twelve Master Jeff Sir...thirteen..."

As Terry lay there crying his thighs reddened with each forceful swipe of Master Jeff's strop. The ruggedly handsome executive clenched his bound hands into fists as he felt swat after swat against his thighs, screaming out the numbers now as they landed.

"AARRRRRHHHH, f-fourteen Master Jeff Sir," Terry screamed out, thinking how there were only ten more swats to endure for this round.

When Master Jeff reached the twenty-fourth swat Terry's face was drenched with tears and his lips were quivering as he called out the number twenty-four, followed by a litany of repeated "Oh God's" over and over.

"Easy my executive, easy does it," Master Jeff said soothingly, stepping behind Terry and running an open hand over the handsome exec's reddened thighs.

Terry blubbered and sobbed under the straps, his entire muscular body quaking. But Master Jeff knew that to stop now would be worse for the spanked guy. Instead, as Terry shook in fear in his bonded position the man he called "Master" shook up the dice. Terry's chin dropped and a look of disbelief filled his handsome face as he saw the second set of double sixes…

"Oh fuck me, oh poor me tonight," Terry whispered as his tears flowed.

"Hmm, seems to me that as tonight is wearing on the fates are turning against you and more in my favor yes Terrance?" Master Jeff asked his charge.

"It, it certainly would seem that way Master Jeff Sir," Terry replied through clenched teeth.

Master Jeff stepped beside Terry, raised the strop and brought it singing and screaming through the air till it connected hard with the backs of Terry's thighs…

"AYYYRRRRR!!!" One…Master Jeff Sir!" Terry squawked and cried.

The executive cried and sobbed but managed to keep the count true. He knew in his heart that if he screwed up the count during this intense part of his training tonight that Master Jeff would not make him start back at the beginning. In some ways the man he called Master was very considerate with him…

As Terry counted and cried his thighs turned redder and redder… his mind wandered back to the first night of his meeting with Master Jeff and the questions that were put to him while he sat wearing just his socks and sipped merlot…

Was it hard for you to cope with your punishments? Yes,

sometimes my stepfather could be kind of cruel when thrashing my ass cheeks. There were times I found it difficult to sit down for the next day or so.

Do you often feel helpless or unsure of yourself? Sometimes.

Do you feel that you panic too easily? No, but I sure did almost panic when you showed me your business card Master Jeff Sir.

Is it overly hard for you to make long term commitments? Not so far.

Do you feel that you are too much of an "over achiever?" Not enough of an over-achiever actually Sir.

Is it hard for you to find solutions too many of your problems? Sometimes, but it sure looks like I might have found a solution to some of my problems tonight.

Do you feel there is now a lack of excitement in your life? Yes, but not anymore, not after meeting you tonight Sir.

Did you have many tantrums while you were growing up? No…because if I did my stepfather took his paddle to me.

Do you usually push yourself beyond your endurance, or until you drop or just can't go any further? No, I seem to know my limits.

Did your parents often help you with your homework? Sometimes.

Is it overly hard for you to start new things, even things you really want to do? Yes, I would have to say that it is indeed getting harder.

Does it bother you to be seen in the nude, even by another male? It's a little unnerving.

Were you considered to be cold or unfriendly, only because you were afraid to open up and express your feelings? No.

What is one of your best assets? On the whole I'm friendly and get along with most everyone.

Do you feel that most of your problems are self induced? I think all my problems are self induced.

Do you often feel that you make a fool out of yourself? No.

When others are getting "rattled" or upset do you remain fairly composed? No, I am just as upset and rattled as they are.

Do you feel that you have a very high tolerance for pain or

endurance? Actually, I think I have an above average tolerance for pain but I am a bit impatient.

Do you like taking part in weird or strange things? I think I am right now doing that.

Do you often get headaches? No.

Do you feel that religion was "over-stressed" in your upbringing? No.

Do you feel that you are now a very religious or spiritual person? Yes, I am at times now.

Were you considered to be a trouble maker in high school or junior high? No, I knew what my step dad would do to me if I were.

Were you often embarrassed or afraid to bring your friends to your house? No.

Do you do many things that you regret doing later? Not really.

Is it often very hard for you to bounce out of depression? No.

Do you find it extremely hard to find solutions to many of your problems? No.

Do you often feel that you are too impulsive? No.

Do you often feel confused or uncomfortable about your sexuality or masculine/feminine persona? Not really. I would like to be more sexual...I'm pretty much heterosexual in my personal life...but have become very stimulated by homosexual activity...mostly dealing with non-consensual stuff like tonight, as I am about to be disciplined and spanked, loss of control. There's a bonding between two men that I can fully understand.

Are your feelings too easily hurt? Yes.

Do you often feel disoriented? Sometimes.

Do you often feel confused or bewildered? No.

Do you often feel that you are too shallow? No.

Were you taught <u>not</u> to trust others? No.

Do you feel that most people don't really listen to you? Yes.

Do you feel there are no real challenges in your life? No, everyday at the brokerage firm I work for is a real challenge.

Were your parents divorced or separated while you were growing up? As I mentioned they were.

Do you feel that you are too introspective? Yes.

Do you feel that whenever you did your best or tried your hardest, your parents would raise their standards and expect more? Yes, mostly my stepfather.

Did your parents believe in "tough love?" My stepfather did.

Do you often feel that you are too opinionated? No.

Do you feel that sibling rivalry was "over-stressed" in your upbringing? No.

Do you like to take chances, even with the odds against you? I think I did that tonight Master Jeff Sir, seeing as you have me sitting here in just my socks.

Do you feel that you are an overly rebellious person? No.

Do you often feel that you are too obsessive? I might be, at times that is.

Is it really hard for you to feel comfortable with your relationships? No.

Do you feel there is now too much pressure on you to perform or to do well? Most definitely, but that pressure is coming directly from me to me.

Do you feel that money or status was "over stressed" in your upbringing? No.

Do you feel that you project a poor image to others on first impression? No.

Do you feel that you need a sharper mind? Yes.

Do you feel that you are often too insensitive to other people's feelings? Sometimes, but mostly at work.

Is it overly hard for you to cope with new situations? No. But this new situation here and now might prove to be a tad hard, we shall see Sir.

Do you feel you should have been punished more while you were growing up? Well, I would have to say yes, seeing as I'm here now and about to be punished. Even though my stepfather dished it out, it seems a part of me was looking for more somehow.

Do you often find yourself in "compromising situations?" Not really.

Do you often wish that you were more spontaneous? A little.

What is one of your worst faults? I demand too much of my underlings at work.

Do you feel that you are too susceptible to peer pressure?
A bit.

Were you often punished when you made mistakes or did poorly at something? Yes, mostly by my step dad.

Do you feel that most people don't take you seriously enough? Yes.

Yes, yes, yes, was the word that Terry was now saying over and over as Master Jeff undid the straps holding him to the "Block" in the soundproofed room. The stropping of the backs of his thighs was over, thankfully and the ruggedly handsome executive's mind was jarred back to the present yet again. Terry had counted well and true and once more proven to his disciplinarian that he could endure a horrific thigh thrashing. It wasn't at every discipline session that Master Jeff walloped the backs of Terry's thighs but the executive figured he needed the dose of harshness this time out. Yes, he was saying to the man he called "Master" in reply to Master Jeff asking him if he was glad that the present discipline session was done.

"Thank you Master Jeff Sir, thank you," Terry panted as Master Jeff rubbed a large ice cube over Terry's reddened ass cheeks and his now crimson thighs.

"Tell me why I'm coating your ass cheeks and thighs with ice my numb nuts executive," Master Jeff ordered.

Still sniveling Terry recited yet another mantra that had been taught to him by the man who had become known to him as his "Master."

"Ice Master Jeff Sir, ice helps to heighten the skins awareness of sensations," Terry said, his fingers clenched into fists as his hands dangled free in front of the "Block" he was still splayed on. "It also acts as a pain reliever in the anti inflammatory sense. It's soothing after the initial rubbing of the hot flesh."

"Very good Terrance," Master Jeff responded and rubbed another ice cube liberally over his charge's ass cheeks and down his thighs, after having deposited what was left of the first ice cube into Terry's hole, getting a real loud sounding yelp from the executive.

"Once you've rubbed ice on the parts of me that you've spanked and paddled already Master Jeff Sir my skin there will be even more sensitive and the pain of the next ass thrashing, if you decide to administer one to me will be more intense," Terry went on and before he could continue Master Jeff stepped in front of him, grabbed a handful of his wavy salt and pepper colored hair and yanked his head upwards.

As the two men looked into each other's eyes Master Jeff said, "Oh you know I plan to administer another ass burning thrashing to those cheeks of yours Terrance."

"Y-yes Master Jeff Sir," Terry whimpered, sopped in sweat at that point.

Master Jeff let go of Terry's hair. Terry hung his head back down and his master resumed rubbing his red flesh with the ice cube.

"Continue telling me the benefits of rubbing ice on your heated skin Terrance," Master Jeff said commandingly.

"Well, once iced a bit there will be less bruising the next time you spank me Master Jeff Sir," Terry said as he lay on the "Block." "Of course an alcohol rub can do the trick at times as well, but because you know that I have to go home to my wife and family I can't risk any telltale scents lingering on my person...and I appreciate your consideration in that area Master Jeff Sir."

Smiling broadly Master Jeff gave one of Terry's reddened ass cheeks a gentle squeeze...

"And lastly Master Jeff Sir, we cannot go on with uninterrupted discipline without a break, a break for both of us," Terry finished. "A break so you can get your second spanking wind and a break for me to revel in and enjoy the stinging pain of what you have put me through thus far...the pain I have endured so far tonight reminds me of my shortcomings of the last two weeks..."

"Very good Terrance, very good indeed..." Master Jeff said and like he did with the first ice cube he inserted the second one into Terry's asshole as well.

Master Jeff nearly laughed out loud at the way his charge's hole seemed to suck in and gulp down what was left of the cube... Terry yelped as his hole slurped up the ice cube and a chill coursed through him...

"Now, before we get to the wooden spoon part of tonight's session perhaps you'd like some cold water to drink," Master Jeff said a few moments later as he helped Terry off the "Block."

"Yes Master Jeff Sir, that sounds wonderful," the sweat sopped high sock wearing executive replied as Master Jeff walked him out of the soundproof room, holding his charge lovingly by the upper arm.

Terry was made to sit on a not so comfortable un-cushioned wooden chair as he sipped down a cool tall glass of water. Being that the chair had no cushion insured that the paddled executive would really feel the sting in his hindquarters as he sat there. Ice had been rubbed on his red and tender sections but when he sat the feeling was less than soothing, as Terry's strict disciplinarian said it should be. Master Jeff reveled in the sight of the well-toned muscular executive as he sat there naked but for his navy blue OTC dress socks, sipping his water and crying. Master Jeff knew at this point in the session that Terry was crying in a mixture of joy at what he had been able to endure thus far and fear at what was coming next as he looked at the wooden spoon on his master's coffee table. As Terry sipped the refreshingly cool water he slowly stopped sweating and his mind wandered once more to the night when he and Master Jeff had first met. Questions, so many questions the man who insisted on being addressed as "Master Jeff" was putting to him it seemed. Master Jeff claimed that these questions and the answers that Terry supplied to them would give him the information he really needed where the executives truest ineptitudes lied. Terry felt more like he was being intensely interrogated…

Do you feel that it is very important to have others look up to you? Yes, definitely, in what I do for a living I need to have leadership qualities.

Did you often "date" or just go out in high school or college? Yes, but I wish I had played the field more.

Do you often find yourself in "out of control" situations? No.

Is it hard for you to control your temper? Sometimes.

Was it hard for you to "break out of your shell" socially? No, I was nudged in the right places.

What is one of the best things that has ever happened to you or what were you most proud of taking part in? Well, I was most proud of getting the promotion where I work to being the manager that I now am and before that I was most proud of having finally moved out of my parent's home. At that time I felt as if I had escaped my stepfather's firm hand. But now it looks like I've traded his firm hand for another…in a way… I'm also most proud of the day I married my wife and of course on the days my children were born.

Do you feel that you are an overly self conscious person? Yes.

If so, what are you most self conscious about? Knowledge of a subject…and sometimes I have trouble remembering names.

Do you feel that you led too much of a sheltered life? No.

Do you get frustrated or uptight much too easily? Sometimes.

Do you often feel that you have no real outlets for your angers? No.

Complete this: I want to be more focused with: my artsy side of my personality.

Are most of your friends: A) Older than you? B) Younger than you? C) About the same age? About the same age.

Do you often find yourself getting drunk or high more often than you are really comfortable with? A little more now it seems...I go to "The Wall Street Local" a little more often than I used to.

Do you want to be more self sufficient or independent? Yes.

What do you usually daydream or fantasize about? Being a vice president, being a great artist and sex.

What are you most sensitive about? What I don't know.

Did you ever run away from home? No, but I did think about it a few times while over my stepfather's knee.

Is it overly hard for you to control your spending? No.

Do you feel that you are too serious or too mature for your age? No.

Did your parents often fight or argue? Well, when my mother was still married to my father they argued a lot. But after she divorced him and married my stepfather they rarely argued or fought.

Do you often feel that others are staring at you? No.

Do you want to have a higher tolerance for pain or endurance than you do now? I think I already have a high tolerance for pain and endurance, being what I was put through by my step dad, but yes, I would like to have an even higher tolerance for it, physically and mentally I would say. (As Terry answered that question he knew in his heart of hearts and at that moment that meeting Master Jeff had been a blessing that night.)

Is it hard for you to assert yourself or speak your mind in tight situations? Sometimes, yes.

Do you usually try not to let others know what you are really thinking? Yes.

Do you feel that you are too much of a showoff or that you brag too much? No.

Is it overly hard for you to really break loose and have a good time? No.

Do you feel that you are too sickly or prone to illness? No.

Is it overly hard for you to feel excited or enthused about things? I do tend to hold in my enthusiasm.

Would you consider yourself to be a "workaholic?" Sometimes, yes I am.

Do you usually "choke" or do very poorly under pressure or stress? No, quite the reverse, because of what my stepfather put me through I think I do better under pressure and stress.

Do you feel that you are too easily offended? Yes.

When you were younger did you have many practical jokes played on you? No.

Complete this: The image I project of myself is: a successful businessman, more so than I really am or more so than I really feel I am.

Do you often feel that you lack tenacity? No.

Do you feel that you are a very competitive person…perhaps too much so? Maybe not competitive enough.

Do you feel that you can be too self absorbed? No.

Were you taught to keep problems to yourself? No.

Do you feel that you are often too cynical? Sometimes I find that I can be, yes.

Do you feel inwardly that you are less masculine than most other males? Not really.

Do you get angry at yourself too much for things beyond your control? Yes.

Do you feel that you could use more peace of mind? Yes, I think my mind could definitely use more peace.

Do you feel that you don't think before you act? No.

Does it really bother you to be interrupted? A bit.

Would you consider yourself to be very unstable? No.

Do you often feel that you are too docile? Yes, sometimes, like tonight. Although I think tonight my being docile is going to work out in my favor.

Does it really bother you to be careless or to make foolish errors or mistakes in front of others unintentionally? Yes.

Do you often do things without thinking about the consequences until it is too late? No.

Do you often feel that you have many self destructive tendencies? No.

Do you often "over" analyze yourself or your actions? No.

Do you feel that you are not living up to your potential? Yes.

Do you often feel tired or run down with low energy levels? Sometimes.

Do you feel that you are an overly nervous, tense, jumpy or high strung person? No.

Do you feel that you are too sexually compulsive? No.

Do you now have a roommate or an apartment mate? Yes.

If so, are you happy with this arrangement? Yes.

Does confrontation generally scare you? No.

Do you feel that you are too much of a loner or anti social? No.

Name one or two problems that you feel you need to be corrected or addressed, but are having trouble dealing with. My procrastination in trying for that VP job at the firm where I work.

Do you want to be more coordinated? Yes.

Are you often bothered by recurring dreams? No.

Do you feel that you are not really prepared to be on your own? No.

Do you like to play practical jokes on people? A bit.

Do you feel that you have done many spiteful things in the past? No.

At what age(s) did you get into the most trouble? Seventeen. When I was seventeen was when my stepfather seemed to thrash me the most with his leather belt.

Were you often afraid to express yourself at home? My true feelings, yes.

Do you feel that punishment and discipline was "over-stressed" in your upbringing? Well yes, the way my stepfather doled it out was sometimes over the top I would say.

Do you ever remember getting spanked, strapped or paddled or beaten (by anyone)? Yes.

Do you feel you were too old the last time you were physically punished? Yes.

How old were you? I was in my teen years and my step dad still thrashed me a few times a week.

Did you often feel you were abused while you were growing up? Sometimes. But in his heart of hearts I really think that my stepfather thought he was doing the right thing by me.

Is it overly hard for you to admit to your mistakes? No.

Do you often wallow in self pity or self hate? No.

Do you feel that you are an overly cautious person? No.

Are you often bothered by a fear of "losing face" or prestige in front of others? Yes.

Did you get into many fights when you were younger? No.

Did you often get into trouble for things you <u>didn't</u> do? No.

Do you feel it is a weakness to <u>show</u> that things are really bothering you? Yes.

Do you suffer from unexplained anxiety attacks? No.

Do you feel that you are too much of an under achiever? Yes, as I have mentioned I feel that I should be a vice president at this point where I work.

Do you feel that you might have an addictive personality? A little.

Are you now or were you ever in a 12 step program? No.

Do you want to be more refined than you are now? No.

Are you bothered by a lack of accomplishment? Yes.

Do you feel your life is going in the direction you planned? Only my married life, my professional life is not.

Were you considered to be weird or strange in high school or junior high? No.

Did you have many nightmares or bad dreams while you were a teenager? Amazingly, no. You would think the way my step dad doled out the punishments that I would have had bad dreams and nightmares, but I never did.

Do you feel your life is now at a turning point? In a way, as of tonight, yes.

What was one of the hardest things you have ever done, or one of your biggest challenges? Well, as of this moment I think just being here and what I'm going to endure will be pretty challenging. As for in the past I would say speaking at a high school rally when I was seventeen years old. I hadn't really wanted to speak at the rally and when I told my stepfather as much he treated me to a really intense ass thrashing. He said it was for my own good and to motivate me for the speech "I WOULD" be making.

Do you feel you need a better sense of values? No.

Are you overly concerned about your appearance? No.

Do you go to the gym or do you workout regularly? Yes.

Were you taught it to be unmasculine to cry or to show emotion? Yes and no. I mean, my stepfather never admonished me for crying when he would pummel my ass with his leather belt. I think it was sort of a given that I would cry, show emotion when he beat me. I mean, it hurt after all. It was more with my teenaged peers that I did not show emotion or cry.

Do you wish you were more diplomatic? No.

Do you feel that you are an overly manipulative person? Not at all. One would think I would be at my place of work, given the position I hold but no, I am not a manipulative man.

Do you feel that you have to prove to others you can do better than them? Yes.

Do you feel that you are more creative than most males your age? Yes.

Were you often mocked or made fun of while you were in high school? No.

Do you often look down upon the actions of your friends? No.

What would you consider to be embarrassing? Losing my pants in a crowd.

Does it really bother you to lose or to do poorly at something? Yes.

What is one of your biggest fears? Being considered a failure.

Do you feel that your pride or ego often gets in your way? Yes.

At this time in your life, what do you feel you need the most? Money, sex and a promotion where I work.

Do you feel that you are an overly sensitive person? Sometimes.

Do you tend to blame others for your own misfortune? No.

Do you often feel disoriented? No.

Do you feel that you are often too eager to please? At times.

Do you often feel guilty and not know why? No.

What do you want to change the most about your present

personality or self image? That I can do it, that I can become a vice president and that I need to work at doing it.

Were you ever in, or did you ever want to be in the military? No.

Do you feel you can handle yourself well in "power" situations? I believe I can, yes.

Do you feel that you need new friends? Sometimes.

What do you want to change the most physically about yourself? Well, I'm in pretty good shape right about now so I suppose I just want to maintain how I look physically, which is why workout often.

Do you feel that you come from a dysfunctional family? Yes and no. I mean, my upbringing was pretty traditional…except for how my stepfather routinely reddened my ass.

Do you feel your short term goals are too high? No.

Do you usually feel sick or upset before a test, a confrontation, a new event, an athletic competition or performance? No.

Do you feel that you are a dull person…perhaps too dull? No.

At this moment, what are you most self conscious or nervous about? What I'll be enduring when I come here for my "sessions" with you Master Jeff Sir…

As Terry recalled answering that last question on the first night he had met "Master Jeff" he realized as he finished his glass of water that there was now a new answer to that particular inquiry. At this moment Terry was most nervous about the thrashing he was going to receive via Master Jeff's large wooden spoon. As he sipped down the last of his cool water the high socked executive's cock churned and throbbed like a thing alive in front of him. His balls dangled low between his thighs, chock filled with his manly fear juices.

"All done Terrance?" Master Jeff asked. "Or would you care for another glass of cold water?"

"Thank you Master Jeff Sir, that's a wonderful offer but I'm done now," Terry replied.

"Good man," Terry's disciplinarian said, sounding prideful. "Now, go and place your glass in the sink and then return here…and when you return bring me my wooden spoon."

"Yes Master Jeff Sir," Terry said and got to his feet, holding his empty water glass in hand.

As Terry padded out of the room Master Jeff noted that the executive's dress socks had slouched down a bit around his calves during their session.

"And unless you want another extra fifty swats you'll pull your socks up Terrance," Master Jeff stated sternly, facing forward as he said it. "You know I want you tidy for our sessions…"

"Y-yes Master Jeff Sir," Terry said and quickly hiked his Gold Toe's up to under his knees after placing his water glass in the sink. "I mean, no Sir Master Jeff Sir, I do not want another fifty extra swats…"

Master Jeff smiled with satisfaction as he heard the water in the sink turned on and then the sounds of Terry washing his water glass…

When Terry returned to the living room Master Jeff was again seated on the spanking couch. Terry's ass cheeks and thighs were red as ripe tomatoes and as much as he hurt and stung back there the executive took a certain pride in what he had endured thus far this evening. As he stepped into the living room, his hard cock pointing the way he stopped midway and stood at soldierly attention before the man he had come to call "Master."

"Master Jeff Sir, I'm ready for the next part of our session," Terry said with the utmost respect.

"Good man Terry," Master Jeff replied. "Bring me my wooden spoon…and you know what else to bring…"

"Yes Master Jeff Sir, I know," Terry said, relaxed his stance of attention and proceeded to open a drawer in a nearby desk.

From the desk Terry produced a deck of everyday playing cards…

With the deck of cards held in hand Terry proceeded next to the coffee table where Master Jeff had his equipment lined up. With his other hand trembling Terry picked up the wooden spoon. This wooden spoon was a few sizes larger than the size of "mom's" stirring spoons and when one was walloped with one of them it hurt about fifty times more. Terry was no stranger to this fact at that point in time. Master Jeff's wooden spoon was about two feet long with the ladle part, or what Terry considered the spanking end about five inches long and two inches wide. After only about five or six strokes from the wooden spoon Terry often found it difficult to keep his butt still and his hands away and it was for those reasons that Master Jeff usually roped his hands behind him…JEEZ.

As Terry stepped to where Master Jeff sat he saw that his

authoritarian was watching him intently. Like earlier with the leather paddle Terry kissed each side of the wooden spoon before handing it to Master Jeff.

"Your wooden spoon Master Jeff Sir," Terry said as he handed Jeff the spoon.

Master Jeff took the spoon from Terry....

Then, Master Jeff nodded "Yes" and Terry knew just what that meant. It was his signal after all. He handed Master Jeff the deck of playing cards and then lowered himself over Master Jeff's lap, his delectable red ass cheeks pointing straight up at the ceiling. Master Jeff marveled at how the crimson hue shone through the hairiness of his charge's butt cheeks...

A few moments later Terry's hands were bound tightly behind him as Master Jeff shuffled the cards a few times.

"Terrance, recite for me why I wallop you with a wooden spoon," Master Jeff ordered.

"Yes Master Jeff Sir," Terry replied, his head dangling at Master Jeff's feet, his wavy salt and pepper colored hair sweaty and dangling in his face at that point. "Ahem, even though the wooden spoon is associated with "Mom's" discipline it really is a very manly type of punishment. Being that you use an oversized wooden spoon makes it a more thorough thrashing than "Mom" used to give."

"Very good Terrance," Master Jeff said and the sound of the cards being shuffled filled Terry with dread as he lay splayed and balanced precariously over his master's lap, his hard cock pressed against Master Jeff's knees.

Terry squirmed a bit on his master's lap and pressed his socked toes hard against the floor in an attempt to maintain better poise. Being in this position reminded him too much of the times when his stepfather used to thrash his ass for him, the main difference here being that his stepfather never tied his hands behind him when he spanked him. At that thought his cock churned all the more. Master Jeff felt Terry's uneasiness at the position he lay in and did a quick maneuver with his legs. A few seconds later Terry felt his hard cock sandwiched between Master Jeff's thighs and then his master used his knees to move Terry's upturned ass a few notches higher.

"Tell me how the amount of swats you receive with my wooden spoon is decided on Terrance," Master Jeff ordered.

"Master Jeff Sir, something like earlier when you used the dice to decide how many swats I would receive this time out you'll be using the deck of cards you trained me to bring you," Terry recited from memory. "The number on the card that you draw will determine how many swats I will receive on my ass cheeks from your wooden spoon. If you draw a king, a queen, or a jack card I will receive twenty swats, as each of the picture cards are worth twenty, your rules. If you draw an ace of diamonds, clubs, or hearts I will receive double the amount of swats shown on the next number card. If you draw an ace of spades I will receive triple the number of swats shown on the next number card. If you draw a Joker card that is in my favor and I will receive no more swats for this session...not even from my stepfather's belt."

"Very good Terrance, very good indeed," Master Jeff said, rubbing Terry's red ass cheeks and sounding like a proud parent as he spoke. "Now tell me my executive, how many times have I ever drawn a Joker card since you started coming to me for sessions Terrance?"

"Master Jeff Sir, you have never drawn a Joker card," Terry intoned and clenched his teeth as he heard the deck of cards being shuffled one last time.

"We'll do three rounds only of this Terrance," Master Jeff said as he drew a card from the top of the deck. "The night is wearing thin at this point..."

"Yes Master Jeff Sir, yes," Terry said, sounding happy and disappointed at the same time.

"I've drawn a ten of clubs Terrance," Master Jeff announced and dropped the card to the floor in front of Terry's dangling face.

"A good number to start with Master Jeff Sir," Terry said out loud and to himself said, "For you but not for me..."

Master Jeff used a lot of shoulder strength this time with Terry. It was one way of making the punishment with the wooden spoon that much more intense.

WHAPPPP WHAPPPP WHAPPPP WHAPPPP was the sound as the rounded end of the large wooden spoon connected hard and harshly with Terry's already reddened behind.

"Count you numb nut executive," Master Jeff ordered.

"OWWWWWWW, y-yes Master Jeff Sir, ONE, TWO, three, four..." Terry squawked loudly.

WHAPPP WHAPPP WHAPPP

"And...five, six, SEVEN, Master Jeff Sir!" the handsome and getting exhausted executive called out.

Terry counted true till Master Jeff reached the tenth swat with the wooden spoon…

As the no-nonsense executive lay splayed with his hands bound behind him across Master Jeff's lap he heard the ominous sound of the deck of cards being shuffled again. Terry clenched his teeth and sweated, a few beads of sweat pooling at the tip of his nose. He pressed his socked toes hard against the floor and his cock churned and throbbed between his master's thighs.

"OOOOOOO Master Jeff Sir!!" Terry bellowed as he felt his man juices boiling in his sweaty sac.

"Getting there finally eh Terrance?" Master Jeff teased his charge as he shuffled the cards.

"UH, y-yes Sir, Master Jeff Sir, I think I can feel it now," Terry squabbled.

"And you know what will happen if you shoot that load and soil my pants don't you?" Master Jeff asked.

"Y-yes Sir, Master Jeff Sir, if, if I shoot my load before you've granted me permission to do so I'll receive a bonus fifty swats with your trusty leather paddle," Terry panted as Master Jeff held up the next card he had drawn. "And I will also have to lick my seed from your pants."

"Very good Terrance, so I'm sure you're now using those self control techniques that I've spanked into you over time, yes?" Master Jeff inquired mockingly, knowing how difficult it was for Terry to hold back shooting his load at this point.

When the topnotch exec had really done well, spank-wise, his elation always made him overly excited in the area of his crotch. It amazed the spanking master how even after all the pain Terry had endured so far he was able to get an erection. Master Jeff again had to wonder how many times a night Terry's wife wanted him. Smiling wickedly Jeff said he had drawn a six of spades.

"Yes Master Jeff Sir, a six of spades," Terry repeated.

Master Jeff raised the large wooden spoon high, pulling back far to gather strength into his shoulder. He then brought the wooden spoon crashing down on Terry's upturned behind.

WHAPPP WHAPPPP

"YOWCCHHH!!!" Terry bellowed loudly through clenched teeth and his bound wrists squirmed in their bondage. "ONE, two, Master Jeff Sir!"

WHAPPP WHAPPP

"RRRRRRRR!!!!! and three and four Master Jeff Sir!" Terry cried out, sniveling and feeling his erection betraying him between Master Jeff's thighs.

"Very good Terrance, but then again, it's not all that difficult to count to six is it now?" Master Jeff chuckled meanly and administered to Terry the last of the six swats, good and hard.

Terry screamed out the numbers five and six and panted madly as Master Jeff shuffled the deck of cards one last time for that particular spanking session. Even though Terry was glad that this area of his punishment would soon be over the most emotionally taxing was yet to come. His cock dribbled pre seed and Terry did his utmost not to lose his load...a bonus of fifty swats he was not looking forward to this night... It had been a rather long night at that he thought.

"A seven of diamonds Terrance," Master Jeff announced. "The cards have been very kind to you tonight I would say..."

"Yes Master Jeff Sir, very kind indeed," Terry said agreeably, recalling sessions with Master Jeff when the cards had not been as kind.

But even though the cards were being kind Terry's entire ass felt like it was the color of a red and overly tomato... He scrunched his ass cheeks together as he felt Master Jeff raise the wooden spoon... This time when Master Jeff walloped his tenderized ass cheeks the sound the wooden spoon made as it connected was more like...

SPLATTTT!!!!

Terry reeled, screamed out the number one and cried like a little kid...

SPLATTTTT!!!

"OHHHHH Master Jeff Sir, t-two..." Terry reeled.

A short while later Master Jeff was done walloping his charge's ass cheeks with the wooden spoon. He commended Terry in a sarcastic tone about how well he had done in holding back shooting his load of pent-up juices. Terry thanked the man he called "Master" and quickly recalled a time when being walloped by Master Jeff using the wooden spoon he "had" shot his load. The topnotch executive could not believe it, seeing as he was in blinding pain at that point...yet he was erect and HAD shot his load, right between his master's thighs as the man held his cock tightly between them. He had cum like a banshee to put it plainly. The first time it had happened Terry Dean Bradshaw could not believe the intensity of his orgasm. It was unlike any gusher he had ever experienced before…even with his very sexually apt wife. Master Jeff had explained that it was his over the top exuberance that had caused Terry to explode his juices. Knowing he had done so well in taking what his master dished out had caused the executive to ejaculate in a mixture of excitement and anguish. Master Jeff also explained how sometimes our emotions fly off the Richter scale, causing us to become erect when we think we could not possibly. It all made sense to Terry, until Master Jeff told him that they would have to work on some self-control techniques where Terry shooting his load while being walloped was concerned. Master Jeff had then ordered Terry to his knees to lick his "seed" from his master's trousers. Terry had never tasted his own cum before. Even when he was a kid and would secretly jack off he was never curious about the taste of his man juices. As he licked his cum off Master Jeff's trousers he discovered that he didn't taste all that bad. He had grinned, secretly thinking of the young lady he had dated when he was in his early twenties and how she had loved drinking from him, as she called it when she would swallow his seed. After he had licked his master's pants clean to his satisfaction Master Jeff then ordered the sock clad lug to his feet and told him that for shooting his load he would suffer an extra fifty swats with the leather paddle. Upon hearing that Terry was prepared to get dressed and leave Master Jeff's apartment but he had committed himself to this man…and inwardly he was only too thrilled to be back over Master Jeff's knees as the man leather paddle swatted him fifty times for shooting his load…

But this time, thanks to Master Jeff's constant attention and spankings Terry had managed to control himself and not shoot his load. His cock however was still rock hard and pulsing. Terry was aching to shoot his load at that point. It had been a long spanking night and the executive had done very well, *he knew*. In his deepest heart of hearts he knew he had pleased his spanking master. His feeling of elation was at an all time high. As Terry stood now with his hands still bound behind him (Master Jeff did not want him rubbing his reddened and stinging ass cheeks just yet, he wanted his handsome executive to revel in the singing sting he was currently feeling) and as Master Jeff gathered him lovingly into his arms as he sobbed Terry's balls felt as if they were dangling just over his OTC dress socks…

"Oh Master Jeff Sir," Terry sobbed, his head resting on his master's shoulder as Jeff held him tight, moving his big hands over and over the executive's huge biceps, stroking his soft salt and pepper colored hair. "TH-thank you Master Jeff Sir!"

Terry allowed his emotions to really flow as he shook, heaved and sobbed in his master's arms.

"Easy Terrance, easy boy," Master Jeff whispered in his charge's ear, his lips grazing Terry's lobe as he spoke. "You did very well this session, very well…and I know you'll do well when we finish very soon…"

As Terry leaned down a tad more Master Jeff moved his hands over Terry's reddened ass cheeks. They were warm to the touch.

"Master Jeff Sir, I'm sorry for my stupidity upon my arrival earlier," Terry blubbered. "That will never happen again Sir!"

"I know, I know," Master Jeff chuckled as he slowly untied Terry's hands, feeling the executive's throbber pressing against him as he did so.

"As you said Sir, I am here for sessions, THERE WILL BE NO MORE EXCUSES or tries for reprieves," Terry went on. "I honestly don't know what I was thinking…"

Once his hands were untied Terry threw his arms around Master Jeff and the two men stood there embracing tightly, Terry still sniveling a bit and whispering "Thank you" over and over. Master Jeff pressed his lips against Terry's tear-soaked cheek and gently kissed him.

"Good man Terrance," he said softly. "But now you must prepare for the final ass thrashing for the night…and then you need to get home to your wife and children…"

Terry said, "Yes Master Jeff Sir, I'm ready…" and as he unfastened himself from his master's embrace Master Jeff kissed him once more on the cheek…

A few minutes later Terry emerged from the bathroom and quickly made his way back to the living room of Master Jeff's apartment. After a good discipline session Master Jeff always allows Terry five to ten minutes of bathroom time. Terry is permitted to do whatever his needs require…except to jack himself off. Master Jeff deems it that Terry must not lose his seed or his desire before his ride home. Terry Dean Bradshaw and Master Jeff have found that Terry's arousal is above average after he has been thoroughly thrashed. When he arrives home after a session with Master Jeff he and his wife go at it like rabbits…to coin Terry's phrase. Of course they go at it in the dark, seeing as Terry would be hard-pressed to try to explain to his wife why his ass and thighs are all red… It is partially that feeling of stinging redness on his ass cheeks (and sometimes his thighs) that seems to thrust Terry forward even more-so as he thrusts into his loving and beautiful wife...

As Terry emerged from the bathroom his mind wandered once more to the first night when he had met the man he would come to call "Master", the man in whose arms he would sob like a baby. The questions that Master Jeff put to him seemed to go on and on, but it was at the end of those questions that Terry Dean Bradshaw would make his life-changing decision. He recalled sitting in front of Master Jeff clad in nothing more than his black nylon OTC dress socks as the questions upon questions were put to him.

Do you often feel that you are too volatile? Sometimes I am, yes.

Do or did any of your parents have a drinking or substance abuse problem? No.

Do you believe in the axiom: "No pain, no gain? I do.

Do you have any tattoos or piercing which you now regret having done? None, I have none.

Do you like being under the control of others or being dominated by others? I uh, I like being in control most of the time, especially where I work. But I will admit to a secret and lusty part of me that wants to be dominated.

Picture yourself doing something creative. What is it? Painting.

If you are gay, are you comfortable about it? I am not gay, but if I were I am sure I would be comfortable about it.

Do you usually do what you are told without questioning? It depends on what I am being told to do.

Do you feel you are too gullible or trusting of others? No, I think I have a good instinct.

Do you often feel that you are too compulsive? No.

What type of situations make you feel uncomfortable? Sitting and answering questions while stripped to my dress socks.

Does competition generally scare you and make you withdraw? No.

Were you considered to be a dork, a nerd or a wimp in high school or junior high? No, being athletic the way I was I was pretty much accepted as one of the guys.

Do you feel that you are in a rut that you cannot get out of easily? Somewhat, but I think as of tonight all that is going to change.

Do you think you are more intellectual or more of a "free thinker" than many your age? A little bit of both I would have to say.

Do you feel your life is now too chaotic or too uncontrolled? A bit uncontrolled, yes.

Do all these questions I am asking you make you feel intimidated, uncertain or apprehensive? No Sir, I feel nervous and on display though the way you have me sitting here stripped to my socks.

Master Jeff told Terry that that was the end of the questioning part of their first session. He put the listing of questions down on the coffee table next to his "spanking" implements. As he spoke Master Jeff stood up and made his way over to his seated charge. Terry had not been told to stand or to get dressed so he simply sat there in his socks.

"Terrance, the next part of this meeting, our consultation if you would is now solely up to you," Master Jeff said and placed a hand on the back of Terry's neck and squeezed gently. "I have decided based on your answers to all those questions that *I want* to be your disciplinarian, your spanking master so to speak. *I want* to take you under my wing and under my paddles and wooden spoons and such. *I want* for you to submit to me Terrance. *I want* you to trust in me. But if you decide to accept me in that manner you must be daring, stoic and brave. Being spanked by me will show your endurance and pride levels, as well as how much you can take mentally and of course physically. This will teach you to think before speaking or acting and to concentrate. I will show you how it is you, AND ONLY YOU that is holding you back from achieving your truest potential in your place of work and career. *If* you give yourself to me in this manner you will learn to think under pressure and you will learn how much it can really bother you to be careless. An example of that is you will be punctual for sessions. If not you will learn lessons and what it means when you are *not* punctual. What I will dish out on you my tall socked and silk underpants executive is PURE BEHAVIOR modification techniques. Some of this is based on military training and/or fear of the unknowns. I gave you an example of fear of the unknowns when I brought you in here blindfolded. Being blindfolded you have already learned to trust me. You have already given yourself to me in the sense of humbling yourself before me in your near total nakedness at this moment. You will learn that real pressure, self induced and other as well as punishment can occur here. Some people who have been spanked by me have cried; some have fainted Terrance Dean Bradshaw."

As Master Jeff recited he gently squeezed the back of Terry's neck and the executive found himself to be rage hard at the cock. He glanced down for a second and saw the pre seed that had oozed from his piss slit and slid down the sides of his throbbing shaft.

"Some have come here, been spanked by me and went through it all without any consequences," Master Jeff went on, taking his hand off the back of Terry's neck and stepping in front of his handsome prize. "It can be done Terrance, if you think and listen, and I assure you my executive, that is a big IF. It can be embarrassing. As you pointed out already you are embarrassed sitting there in just your socks. But the reaction that I see in your erection shows me excitement, perhaps a certain fear as well. Many men find themselves erect and pulsing when feeling fear. It can also be a little painful what I will do to you here, perhaps *very* painful at times, depending on how much discipline I feel you are in need of when at any of your sessions. I can see from the look on your face that you are also very curious Terrance."

For the briefest of moments Master Jeff ceased speaking, stood close to his seated charge and gently took Terry's chin in his fingers and thumb. Breathlessly he asked, "So tell me Terrance, tell me my handsome executive that fate seems to have brought to me tonight, *tell me*, are *you* willing to take the risk and challenge?"

"I'm willing Master Jeff Sir," Terry whispered and the tears in his eyes flowed down his cheeks.

Terry abruptly stood up and he and Master Jeff embraced tightly…both men knowing that a new and very special camaraderie, comradeship and friendship had just been born in that room…

"Let's go to the spanking couch Terrance," Master Jeff whispered as they hugged.

"Yes Master Jeff Sir, yes," Terry sniveled.

As Terry recalled that first trip to the spanking couch his mind was again jarred back to the present moment as he once more made his way to the spanking couch…where Master Jeff was seated and awaiting his charge. Terry padded on his navy blue socked feet to the coffee table where the man he called "Master" had his spanking implements lined up. It was time for the final ass thrashing…and it would be with Terry's stepfather's leather belt that he would suffer that final thrashing of the night. It was always the most emotional of all the thrashings as Terry's mind wreaked havoc on him with the memories of how his stepfather used to discipline him. Back then when he was a teenager Terry felt that the harsh discipline was a bit over the top…a bit not needed. But now, as an adult Terry knew in his heart of hearts how much he needed the kind of therapy that Master Jeff subjected him to. With his hand trembling Terry picked up his stepfather's leather belt and brought it to Master Jeff. For the briefest of seconds Terry saw his stepfather sitting on the couch instead of Master Jeff.

"Good man Terry," Master Jeff said as Terry stood before him with the belt in hand, his muscular chest heaving up and down and his erection pulsing as he fought his tears.

"Master Jeff Sir," Terry sniveled in a mixture of fear and joy. "I bring to you my stepfather's leather belt. It was the instrument of my punishment when I was a younger man, punishment that my stepfather doled out on me. Now it will be you using that same leather belt… Master Jeff Sir…"

Terry's erect cock stared Master Jeff in the face as he listened to his charge recite his litany. Terry then kissed the leather belt and handed it to his master…

Master Jeff gestured toward his lap and Terry lay himself down across it, his red ass pointing straight up at heaven…

WHAPPPP WHAPPP WHAPPP WHAPPPP was the stinging sound that filled the air and consumed Terry's already reddened ass cheeks as Master Jeff administered the final punishment for the evening. As Terry screamed, cried and counted he recalled how on the first night he met Master Jeff he had found himself in the same exact position, splayed over his master's lap, his delectable ass cheeks in the air…and being thoroughly and well spanked. It seemed in the ruggedly handsome executive's mind the two nights had come together on this night…and now as he was thrashed with his stepfather's leather belt memories of that man as well filled Terry Dean Bradshaw's mind…

As Master Jeff administered the final ass thrashing to Terry Dean Bradshaw's reddened behind the executive's mind once more returned to the first night he had met his "master."

"Yes Master Jeff Sir," Terry repeated again as Master Jeff sat down on the spanking couch and pointed to his lap.

"Over my knees and lap Terrance," Master Jeff said. "That is the position you will always assume here at the spanking couch," Master Jeff instructed the erect executive.

"Yes Master Jeff Sir," Terry said as his tears stopped their flow for the moment. "There will be other positions you will assume in this place, my apartment, but for the moment the one I want you in is over my knees and lap. The other positions you will learn as time goes on."

But as he was about to splay and humble himself over Master Jeff's lap Master Jeff held up a hand, halting Terry.

"Hand me my round leather paddle Terrance," Master Jeff said commandingly, pointing at the lined up items on the coffee table he sat in front of. "And before you hand it to me I want you to show the paddle your respect and thanks by kissing it on both sides."

"Yes Master Jeff Sir," Terry responded.

The stripped to his black socks and erectly throbbing executive leaned over and picked up the round leather paddle. As he bent over slightly Master Jeff took in the sight of Terry's well-shaped delectable ass globes. A chill crept up the spanking master's spine as Terry's crack gaped a bit. He watched as Terry picked up the leather paddle, held it in front of his face and kissed both sides of it. Master Jeff smiled with satisfaction as Terry handed him what would be the first instrument of his discipline.

"Now Terrance, for tonight I will spank you only with the leather paddle," Master Jeff said, pointing at his lap.

"Yes Master Jeff Sir," Terry said and got himself situated over Master Jeff's lap, his arms spread out in front of him, the palms of his hands pressed against the floor, his socked toes pressed against the floor behind him.

"Your job now is to count off the swats you receive," Master Jeff went on, rubbing the paddle against Terry's upturned ass cheeks.

"Yes Master Jeff Sir," Terry said.

"I will administer to you fifty consecutive swats for tonight Terrance," Master Jeff said. "This will be our getting to know each other spanking for you. If you jumble up the count by skipping a number or if you repeat a number we'll start back at the beginning."

"Yes Master Jeff Sir, I understand Sir," Terry piped up.

"Now, place your hands behind you and balance yourself on my lap you numb nut executive," Master Jeff said and Terry took a deep breath before doing as he had been told.

"You will always lay across my lap with your hands and arms crossed up behind you Terrance," Master Jeff stated. "If you try to move your hands down to rub your ass cheeks as I redden them I will proceed to tie your hands behind you. Is that clear?"

"It, its clear Master Jeff Sir," Terry replied and as his cock slid between Master Jeff's thighs he felt his cum churning in his tightened up balls.

Master Jeff chuckled as he squeezed his thighs around Terry's erection...

"Begin counting Terrance, and be true in your count," Master Jeff said and raised his paddle.

WHAPPP WHAPPP WHAPPP WHAPPP

"AWWWWW SHIT, ONE, TWO, three, and four, Master Jeff Sir," Terry called out loudly, clenching his big hands into tight fists.

WHAPPP WHAPPP WHAPPP

"OOOOHHHH, I-I'm really bein' spanked here, JEEZ!!" Terry garbled throatily, a bit of triumph sounding in his voice. "f-five, six... seven...and eight..."

"And forty-two more to go Terrance," Master Jeff said gleefully and raised his leather paddle.

"Yes Master Jeff Sir, YES SIR!" Terry responded and received the next five swats, each one harder than the one before it.

Terry's cock throbbed between his new master's thighs and as he squirmed on Master Jeff's lap and sang out the numbers he knew he would shoot his load. He wondered what the punishment for shooting his load between his master's thighs would be...

As time went on Terry found out that shooting his load between his master's thighs would mean an extra fifty swats for that session... with the stinging leather paddle no less. Over time Master Jeff explained to Terry that his excitement over having done well and endured a hard spanking session was what made Terry erect and what caused him to cum as well. Master Jeff spanked self control into his charge where this was concerned so that Terry did not shoot his load while being spanked, rather he was taught to hold his seed till he arrived home to his wife...just as he would now in the present...

As Terry recalled that first night, as he recalled his first spanking from Master Jeff his mind was jarred back to the present as he reeled out through clenched teeth the number "Fifty."

After being thoroughly thrashed fifty times with his step father's leather belt Terry stood and embraced Master Jeff. The two men hugged tightly, Terry's head resting on his master's shoulder as he cried and heaved in his arms.

"Good man Terrance, good man indeed," Master Jeff cooed gently in his charge's ear. "You did very well tonight Terrance; know that my executive, *you did very well...*"

"Thank you Master Jeff Sir, thank you, *thank you...*" Terry sniveled and hugged his master tighter as he looked at his step father's leather belt where it lay back on the coffee table. "Thank you so much Sir..."

"Let's get you some soothing aloe cream yes?" Master Jeff asked his charge and gave Terry's red as a ripe tomato ass a squeeze.

"Yes Sir Master Jeff Sir, lets do that," Terry replied and with his hands crossed behind his back followed his master like an obedient puppy to the bathroom.

In the bathroom Terry bent over and grabbed his socked ankles, putting his reddened ass cheeks and thighs on ample display for Master Jeff. Terry stood mortified and docilely still as the man he called "Master" rubbed a liberal amount of unscented aloe cream over his thrashed and wounded ass cheeks and thighs.

"Feels good Terrance?" Master Jeff asked as he reveled in his present chore, rubbing his aloe creamed hands over and over Terry Dean Bradshaw's bottom and over his delectable thighs.

"Yes Master Jeff Sir, very soothing, but I can still feel the sting," Terry replied. "And that's good Master Jeff Sir. Feeling the sting will remind me of my shortcomings and ineptitudes..."

"Precisely Terrance, precisely," Master Jeff said and just for the fuck of it slid an aloe cream slicked finger into Terry's bunghole.

Terry gripped his socked ankles tighter and gasped...

A short while later Terry was dressed in his suit, tie and wingtip shoes. He hugged Master Jeff one more time, said he would see him in two weeks and then left the apartment...

On his way home on the subway even though there was ample seating Terry Dean Bradshaw opted to stand...

A Boner Book

I FINALLY SUBMIT

Author's Note: In my first book "The Executive Guide to Foot Fetishism and Office Discipline" I introduced readers to my friend and spanking master, "Master Jeff" in the story "A Spanking Good Time." That story was a fantasy of Master Jeff's. The story you just read, "Terry's Appointment" was a fantasy of both Master Jeff's and mine. The next story/fantasy, "I Finally Submit" shows a more sadistic, rawer side of Master Jeff. The following story was also inspired by the book "That Day at the Quarry", written by Tom Shaw. It was that book that many of my readers know started me on this more sadistic/erotic writing genre. The story shows how true friends can really trust each other even in the most erotic mixed with horrific settings where they explore each other's fantasies.

The Story

When I finally agreed to allow my friends Master Jeff and Bill to work me over on a Saturday afternoon at Master Jeff's apartment we all met a week before the day to have lunch. During lunch we discussed how we would play out this erotic fantasy of dominance and submission, talking about what we would and would not do. Or more precisely what *they* would do and not do to me. (Right...) I agreed to intense spankings in my underpants with the backs of their hands and leather paddles. I agreed to allow them to tie me up, to torture my nipples and jack me off till my cock was sore and then some. I promised that I would lick and service Bill's black nylon dress socked feet (my all time weakness) in between being spanked. My submissive nature would truly be put to the test on the arranged date. Master Jeff and Bill said they would respect my limits and that a safe word would be agreed upon. (Right...I would learn that Master Jeff can be very sadistic and meanly clever in this area of play...) With a grin on his face Master Jeff said that if I wanted them to stop working me over at anytime all I would have to say is "Please stop." We proceeded to have lunch and talk about why I had finally agreed to all this erotic torture. As we talked my cock churned in my jeans, hard and throbbing let me tell you. Master Jeff had wanted a chance to work me over since Bill had introduced me to him a little over two years ago at that point. I told them that I had played the role of the master many times in discipline sessions with Bill and wanted now to explore my submissive side. Master Jeff looked at me fiendishly across the table and said that he would be glad to assist me in exploring my submissive side...all afternoon on the following Saturday. For a second I thought about backing out of it but quickly told myself that these two men were my friends and that we would all have a great time. Sure, they would have a great time. I would scream and sweat and cry my fucking guts out...as I would find out in a week's time. Master Jeff instructed me not to jack off for the entire week. He said that he wanted me good and primed, real horny when the day arrived. He went on to tell me how I would learn the thin line between pain and pleasure. He told me how to dress and then we finished our lunch. As the week went by I thought about the upcoming Saturday afternoon everyday. As I thought about my two buddies working me over my cock would get instantly hard in my pants. I was glad that I usually wore pleated dress pants to work everyday, it hid the hard-on I was sporting most of the time...

Saturday Afternoon

I arrived at Master Jeff's apartment at the appointed time of twelve PM on the dot. I walked in wearing blue jeans, a white tee shirt and black construction boots. Master Jeff dressed in black jeans, black construction boots and a black tee shirt greeted me at the door and as he closed the door behind us I saw Bill sitting on a chair in the living room. Bill was looking real sexy and scantily dressed in just a pair of teal green boxer briefs, a pair of OTC (over the calf) black ribbed nylon socks, and slip-on loafers. At the sight of Bill my breath caught in my throat. He looked great dressed like that, totally sexy. As I was about to walk over to him and suck one of his oversized nipples a few times Master Jeff grabbed me by an arm, halting me. I looked at him as he held me tightly by my arm. He told me I had just one chance and one chance only to back out of our deal. If not, I was theirs for the afternoon. Suddenly, my friend Master Jeff didn't look so friendly anymore. He was playing his part very well and I have to admit he had me feeling scared. I saw the leather paddle on the couch along with a pair of handcuffs.

"Okay…I'm ready…" I said slowly, my cock growing what I call "fear" hard in my pants.

Master Jeff told me that I knew what to do. We had discussed it the week before after all. Master Jeff and Bill watched as I stripped down to my white briefs, black construction boots and white sweat socks. They looked me over lustfully, commenting on my muscular body as if I weren't right there in front of them. I then stood with my hands behind me and looked straight ahead as they came over to me. I was not to look at them as they looked me over. I was now their property. They squeezed my nipples, squeezed my ass cheeks through my briefs and slapped my ass a few times.

"He looks scared," Bill said, sounding concerned.

"Good, he should be," Master Jeff said mockingly and slapped my ass hard, the sound resounding in the living room, the sting making me yelp. "He's about to have an afternoon he'll never forget…"

I continued staring straight ahead, knowing they were just playing their roles…as I was playing mine. They both gave my nipples a few good sucks, driving me wild, making my cock grow harder in my briefs.

"Kiss Bill's feet and lick his socks," Master Jeff said directly into my ear and slurped my earlobe.

"Yes Sir Master Jeff Sir!" I replied heartily.

I slid down to my knees and leaned forward on them, wrapping my hands around Bill's ankles. (For the record here I love licking and worshipping Bill's feet even when he is the slave in our scenes together.) I kissed Bill's loafers and then ran my tongue slowly up and over his socks, kissing them a few times on the way up, sniffing them heavily, and loving the funky odor. As I worshipped Bill's feet Master Jeff gave my raised ass a few good whacks with the leather paddle and mocked me by calling me a puny slave. I yelled "OWWWWW" as I continued worshipping Bill's feet.

"Now kiss his underpants," Master Jeff said to me sternly.

I sat up on my knees, grabbed Bill's thighs and pressed my lips against his silk boxer briefs. I kissed them all over as Bill moaned in pleasure and Master Jeff whacked my ass again with the leather paddle. Bill caressed the back of my neck as I kissed his underpants over and over, pressing my lips hard against the outline of his erection in them.

"Okay, back on your feet with your hands behind you!!" Master Jeff shouted at me commandingly.

I pulled myself quickly to my feet, yelled out "Yes Master Jeff Sir" and crossed my hands behind my back. I stared straight ahead, but wanted so much to look at Bill. I wanted so much to lick his socks and boxer briefs again. I wanted to kiss Master Jeff's boots as a way of saying "thank you" to him for all of this. But those things would be my rewards when my masters felt I had earned it.

"Lock his hands behind him," Master Jeff ordered Bill.

"Yes Sir," Bill replied and picked up the handcuffs.

Bill stepped behind me and locked the (cold) metal handcuffs around my wrists.

"How does it feel to be handcuffing him Bill?" Master Jeff asked Bill and squeezed one of my nipples hard. "God knows the little bastard did it to you enough times over the years."

"I know…" Bill said and kissed me on the back of my neck. "It sure does seem like the tables have turned."

As they spoke they went on squeezing my nipples and ass cheeks, sending chills through me. I was feeling a little scared by then because I knew there was no turning back now. When Bill had cuffed me a feeling of utter helplessness had consumed me. Master Jeff told Bill to go and sit down on the couch. Bill would have the honor of spanking me first. Bill sat down on the couch and Master Jeff grabbed me by both arms.

"You ready Hot shot?" he asked me tauntingly, squeezing my biceps hard. "Well, even if you're not ready *it's time*. The say has arrived! You are ours! Got that safe word ready in case you need it?"

"Y-yes Sir…" I whispered, my mouth feeling dry.

Master Jeff let go of my arms, took a ball-gag out of his pocket and quickly tied it over my mouth.

"RRRRRUUMMMFFF…" I garbled, feeling confused.

As Master Jeff walked me over to Bill I wondered how the hell I would be able to say the safe word with that damned ball-gag in my mouth. At that moment I realized there was to be no safe word. The two fuckers were going to work me over till *they* had decided I had had enough. Obviously they had planned this. Shit, what had I gotten myself into??? Master Jeff laid me across Bill's lap and Bill ran the palm of his hand over my ass cheeks. Master Jeff told Bill that they would each give me ten hard whacks with the backs of their hands with my briefs still pulled up first. Then, they would give me ten hard whacks each with the backs of their hands with my briefs pulled down. After that if my ass was red enough I would be allowed to worship Bill's feet, his underpants, and maybe be allowed to suck one of his bulbous nipples for a few seconds. After that I would be spanked again, this time with the leather paddle on my bare ass. As I listened to all this my eyes filled with tears of fear and dread. I was also wondering when I would be jacked off in between all the abuse I was about to endure.

"RRRUMMMMFFF…" I snarled at Master Jeff, my head raised slightly and turned toward him.

"That didn't sound like the safe word to me Asshole," he said to me meanly. "Okay Bill, start spanking the bastard."

Bill raised his hand and brought it down hard on my ass.

"MMMFFFFF!!!" I cried out, my head dangling by his feet.

He spanked my ass again and God how I wished I could lick Bill's socks at that moment. He spanked me hard two times in a row and I wailed in pain as he whacked me again. That was five so far. With each blow though Bill whacked me harder and harder. I never knew that Bill had it in him to be sadistic at all. When he reached the tenth whack I was already shaking and Master Jeff hauled me roughly to my feet by my upper arms. Seconds later Master Jeff was sitting on the couch with me over his lap, his big palm on my ass.

"How did that feel Bill?" Master Jeff asked Bill and whacked my ass hard, getting a good loud muffled yelp out of me. "Did you enjoy giving it to him for a change?"

He whacked me a second time, harder this time. I screamed into the ball-gag.

"Yes, payback sure is a bitch," Bill said with a wicked looking smile. "Especially for him today…"

Master Jeff whacked me two more times and I ranted into the gag.

"Still, it seems unfair to have gagged him," Bill said and Master Jeff whacked me a fifth time.

I nodded my head up and down, agreeing with Bill, and Master Jeff whacked me sixth time, hard. I screamed in pain.

"Unfair to have gagged him?" Master Jeff asked Bill and whacked my ass a seventh time. "Was it fair all those times he blindfolded you for his fun?"

"Are we going to blindfold him too?" Bill asked Master Jeff.

"If we want to, sure," Master Jeff said and whacked my ass an eighth and ninth time. "We can do *whatever the fuck we want with him*...he's ours for the afternoon..."

Master Jeff brought his hand up high and gave me the tenth and hardest whack.

"RRRMMFFF!!!" I wailed and for a moment I thought Bill looked like he felt sorry for me.

God knows I was feeling sorry for myself at that moment. They pulled me to my feet again and ran their hands over my muscular chest and squeezed my pecs hard, causing them to get a little red. Master Jeff bit one of my nipples as Bill squatted in front of me and kissed my briefs a few times. It seemed both Bill and I have an underwear fetish, among other fetishes. I whimpered into my gag and my cock pounded like crazy in my briefs. I looked at Master Jeff beseechingly, begging him to read my mind and take the damned gag out of my mouth...no such luck though because he ordered Bill to get to his feet. It was time to pull down my briefs and whack my bare ass. They pulled my briefs down in the back and made jokes about how hairy my rear end was. They pulled on some of the hairs on my ass cheeks and squeezed and pinched it hard a few times. As I stood there whimpering in fear Bill kissed my neck.

"Okay, this time I go first," Master Jeff said anxiously and sat down on the couch.

Bill laid me across Master Jeff's knees and Master Jeff raised his hand high. He brought it down fast, whacking my ass cheeks hard.

"RRRMMFFFF!!!" I cried out loudly.

I squirmed on Master Jeff's lap as he whacked me hard two more times, holding me in place with his other arm around me.

"Wow, his ass cheeks are sure turning red quick," Bill commented. "I love the way the redness shines through his forest of hairy ass."

"Sure is," Master Jeff said and whacked me hard a fourth time, reddening my ass cheeks some more. "I suppose he'll be getting his reward soon."

Master Jeff whacked me hard a fifth and sixth time and then gave my ass cheeks a hard squeeze each. I whimpered loudly and tears were already streaming down my cheeks. I was crying in a mixture of pain and the fact that two of my best buddies in the world had shanghaied me into this situation.

"Do you think you're ready to worship Bill's socks and boxer briefs?" Master Jeff asked me tauntingly and whacked me hard a seventh time. "It's why I had him strip down the way he is, just for you."

I nodded that I was and Master Jeff relentlessly whacked my ass an eighth and ninth time. My ass cheeks were tingling and in searing pain as Master Jeff administered to me the tenth whack…the hardest one yet. I screamed in a high pitched tone of voice behind the ball-gag and when I was yanked to my feet I saw that Bill was looking at me sympathetically. There wasn't much he could do though at that moment. I had agreed to all of this and Master Jeff was in charge… and he obviously loved every moment of my torment. It was why he had gagged me after all. He was taking no chances whatsoever on my backing out of this. In seconds I was lying across Bill's lap again, my naked hairy ass a ready target for his hand.

"Hurry up and give him ten good hard ones," Master Jeff said encouragingly to Bill. "I want to get started on using the leather paddle on him."

Bill raised his hand and brought it down hard on my ass.

"RRRMMFFFF…" I cried looking longingly at Bill's feet as my head dangled there.

He whacked me again, harder this time. Then a third time. When he gave me the fourth whack I screamed in pain and he simply whacked me a fifth time. If Bill was feeling sorry for me at all it sure wasn't showing at the moment. He whacked me hard a sixth and seventh time. My ass cheeks felt like they were already on fire when he whacked me an eighth time. I glanced up and saw that Master Jeff was holding the leather paddle in his hand. He was grinning at me fiendishly. I looked back down, tears streaming down my face. Bill whacked my ass the ninth and ten times…hard. I reeled into my ball-gag. That done they had each given me a total of twenty whacks so far, tallying forty all together. And I was in for a shit-load more. They pulled me to my feet and looked me over as I stared straight ahead.

"Doin' okay Asshole?" Master Jeff asked me and squeezed one of my nipples as Bill sucked my other nipple, both of them sending searing sensations through me. "Enjoying yourself so far? It's all what you came here for after all…"

I knew that the verbal abuse Master Jeff was heaping on me was only part of the scene. He really didn't mean it when he called me an asshole or a bastard…although I was feeling like an asshole at that moment for getting myself into all this. Master Jeff was truly playing his role to the utmost of perfection. I could only nod in response to Master Jeff's questions and he ran the leather paddle over my ass cheeks.

"Boy oh boy are you in for it now shit-head," Master Jeff said to me. "But we did promise you something too I suppose."

Bill sat down on the chair and crossed one of his legs. He slipped one of his loafers off his socked foot and Master Jeff took the ball-gag out of my mouth. I looked at Master Jeff somewhat angrily.

"Not a word Shit-head," Master Jeff said to me sternly. "If I hear *any* complaints out of that mouth of yours I'll give you twenty hard whacks with this paddle as a bonus round…"

I looked at him, humbled quickly, and gulped hard. He had really taken control of me it seemed. He then told me to get myself over to where Bill was sitting and to have a few moments of some fun. I walked over to Bill and knelt down in front of his crossed leg. I leaned forward and sniffed the inside of Bill's loafer that was on the floor. It smelled heavenly in that shoe, nice and musty and manly. Then, I sat up on my knees and licked Bill's socked foot, drooled over his toes and sucked them hard as I sucked up my saliva. Bill moaned contentedly. The aroma and pheromones that Bill emanated from his feet through his nylon dress socks sent me into orbit. I loved the feel of the black nylon in my mouth and the way Bill wiggled his toes in there as I sucked them. Obviously I loved the taste of Bill's funky socked feet. I kissed his foot all over and licked his sock as much as I could because I knew that Master Jeff was anxious to get started spanking me again. Bill ran a hand through my hair soothingly and at his touch I knew at that moment that he was indeed feeling sorry for me. Hell, I was feeling sorry for myself at that moment. A few more minutes passed and then Master Jeff ordered me to my feet. I instantly did as I was told. He stepped behind me, grinned and tied the ball-gag back over my mouth, wedging it into my craw as he did so.

"Man, are you in for it now…" Master Jeff said and squeezed my arms tight, practically lifting me off the floor.

I shuddered and my heart pounded at sixty miles an hour in my chest. Bill put his shoe back on and Master Jeff told him to sit on the couch. Bill, like me, did as he was told. My cock was rock hard with fear as Master Jeff laid me across Bill's lap.

"MMMMFFF…" I whimpered softly.

I was shaking all over as Master Jeff handed Bill the leather paddle.

"Okay Bill, he's going to scream louder than before when we whacked him with the backs of our hands," Master Jeff said to Bill. "Seeing as his ass is already reddened that just makes sense. But don't worry; just give him all you've got."

"Yes Sir!!" Bill replied and raised the paddle.

I closed my eyes tight and Bill brought the paddle down hard on my bare ass. I screamed in agony. He whacked me a second and third time. The leather paddle didn't hurt so much as it burned my ass cheeks intensely. When Bill whacked me a fourth time I raised the front part of my body and reeled in pain, looking at Master Jeff pleadingly as he watched the spectacle in front of him…loving every moment of it as I was erotically tortured. The muscles in my arms flexed involuntarily and my chest and pecs bounced. Master Jeff seemed to like the sight of that I'm glad to say. Bill whacked me a fifth time and I laid myself back down over his lap. Master Jeff leered at me as Bill whacked me hard a sixth time. I was crying big tears by the time Bill got around to the seventh and eighth whacks. Shit, that leather paddle had to be the ultimate device of torture when it came to spanking a poor guy's ass cheeks. I was in so much pain that even my erection had shriveled up real soft. I could not fucking believe it. Bill whacked me the ninth and tenth times… VERY HARD. Jeez, just five swats with a leather paddle are enough to make a guy rant and scream in pain. But my two buddies weren't going to be that stingy where the leather paddle was concerned. I was going to be administered to very generously with that damned leather paddle. When they pulled me to my feet my two buddies had to hold me steady by my arms as I was shaking and crying uncontrollably. I looked at them beseechingly, begging them to stop now. But Master Jeff and Bill simply ran their hands over my chest, squeezed my big nipples a few times and assured me that I was doing very well so far. Actually I wasn't doing well at all. My ass cheeks felt like they were literally on fire. Bill gave one of my nipples a few gusty sucks and squeezed my red ass cheeks before Master Jeff ordered me across his knees…with no help from Bill. Master Jeff sat down on the couch and the two men watched as I laid myself across Master Jeff's lap, making my ass a ready target for him. He picked up the leather paddle and ran it over my reddened ass cheeks.

"Okay Asshole, now you're going to feel REAL pain!" Master Jeff said and raised the paddle.

He brought the paddle down hard on my ass cheeks. I roared in pain and Master Jeff quickly whacked me a second and a third time. Tears streamed down my face, snot was accumulating in my nose, I was sweating like a stuck pig and I was starting to feel dizzy. As Master Jeff whacked me relentlessly a fourth and fifth time I looked up at Bill in agony. I was praying he would ask Master Jeff to stop. Master Jeff whacked me a sixth time…a seventh time. I screamed louder and louder in pain, trying to make them realize that I had had enough…much more than enough actually. But for Master Jeff the fun was just starting. And the fun starred me as his unwitting actor. I realized that they hadn't blindfolded me yet and I hadn't been jacked off once yet…something I would have really appreciated at that moment. Master Jeff whacked me an eighth and ninth time, saving the tenth and hardest for last. He administered the tenth whack and then ordered me to my knees. I slid off his lap, crying like crazy and kneeled on the floor, my head down, whimpering and slobbering against my ball-gag. The two men stood over me. All I could see were two pairs of feet in front of me, Bill's clad in his loafers and nylon socks and Master Jeff's in his construction boots.

"We've humbled him pretty well so far," Master Jeff said to Bill.

"Do you still want to give him more?" Bill asked Master Jeff.

"Hell yes, the afternoon is young," Master Jeff replied. "But let's give him some water in the meantime. He sure looks like he can use it."

So far I had suffered a total of sixty whacks to my ass cheeks… and I knew there were a lot more coming…

A few minutes later I was sitting on the chair with my briefs pulled back up over my reddened ass cheeks. The ball-gag was out of my mouth and my hands were still cuffed behind me. Bill held a tall glass of cool water to my trembling lips and I sipped it slowly, enjoying the taste of the cold clear liquid as it slid down my throat. My shaking had subsided some and Bill gingerly wiped away my tears with a small towel, kissing me on the face in between that chore.

"You can speak if you want to, but only temporarily," Master Jeff said to me, squeezing my shoulder reassuringly.

I looked up at Master Jeff in anger.

"You bastard," I said to him. "You never intended for me to have a safe word. Your only intention was to get me here and work me over…*big fucking time.*"

I clenched my teeth and shook my cuffed hands behind me.

"Well, now that we have that bit of information out of the way I won't need to gag you for the next few rounds of spanking that you're in for Asshole," Master Jeff said. "And yes, you're right; I have waited a long time for this. Too long, so I intend to savor and enjoy every minute of it." He squeezed one of my nipples hard, twisting the fuck out of it.

"OWWWWW!!!" I screamed. "Fucker…"

"I'm going to make you scream so loud you won't believe it…" Master Jeff said, looking at me menacingly.

I sipped some more water as Master Jeff squeezed my shoulder again. We were all playing our parts to the hilt, especially me. After I was done drinking the water Master Jeff and Bill pulled me to my feet and ran their hands over me again, pinching my nipples and squeezing and twisting them hard, squeezing my ass cheeks and slapping them a few times each. That was pretty mean I thought, seeing as my ass cheeks were already stinging. When Bill reached into the front section of my briefs and gave my balls a hard squeeze I yelped loudly and nearly jumped into the air. Master Jeff ordered Bill to sit down on the chair and to get one of his shoes off. Bill again did as he was told and Master Jeff ordered me to get busy. I knelt in front of Bill as he crossed his leg and I hungrily licked his socked foot, sucked at his toes and kissed and kissed his leg up to his knee. I pressed my nose against Bill's boxer briefs and took a deep and hearty sniff of them. They were scented with sweat and piss with some pre cum thrown in for good measure. Bill's Irish cock was hard as a rock in the silky boxer briefs. He was enjoying all this. It was partially his revenge after all. When Master Jeff decided I had relaxed enough he ordered me to my feet again. I instantly did as I was told. Moments later I was kneeling on the chair with my stomach area against the back of the chair. Master Jeff had taken the handcuffs off my wrists and tied my wrists in front of me to the top of the chair. (I did not try to resist while my hands were free. I was too weak for one thing, and I had agreed to all of this…and I NEVER go back on my word.) As Master Jeff tied a black cloth blindfold over my eyes Bill was squatting behind me, kissing my red ass cheeks, which were already exposed for the next round of spanking.

"Feeling okay?" Master Jeff asked me and kissed my arm.

"I'm scared Master Jeff," I replied sheepishly.

"Good, you should be," Master Jeff said mockingly. "Bill, hand me the riding crop."

"Master Jeff, no!!" I pleaded, tears flooding my eyes behind the blindfold.

"Oh my beautiful prisoner, you are in for it now..." Master Jeff said mockingly and ran the tip of the riding crop against my ass cheeks and over my ass crack...teasing it.

"God almighty, please, no...not the riding crop..." I whimpered. "*Bill...*"

"Ten whacks Asshole," Master Jeff said. "Bill, suck his tits and hold him tight while I work on this hairy butt of his with the riding crop.

Bill stepped in front of me, grabbed my arms and slurped one of my nipples into his mouth.

"OOOOOOO yeah..." I moaned.

But then, Master Jeff whacked me with the riding crop, straight across my buttocks.

"AAAYYRRRRR!!!" I screamed loudly and almost pitifully.

Bill sucked my nipple harder as Master Jeff whacked me a second and third time, harder with each blow.

"OHHHHHH, *you fuckers!!*" I screamed in agony.

Master Jeff whacked me a fourth and fifth and sixth time. He asked me if I was enjoying my erotic experience. With tears soaking my blindfold all I could do was shake in fear and cry like a fucking baby.

Being blindfolded makes it worse eh Hot shot?" Master Jeff asked me and whacked my ass a seventh time. "Makes you really concentrate on the pain you're receiving."

I wailed in tortured agony as he whacked me three more times, completing the ten whacks. That made seventy whacks all totaled so far that I had suffered that afternoon.

"He's really hurting," Bill said after taking his mouth off my nipple.

Bill wrapped his arms around my upper body and caressed the back of my neck, soothing me a bit.

"Master Jeff, he never hurt me the way you're hurting him," Bill said and kissed my cheek.

As Bill spoke I cried more and more, hoping that Master Jeff would decide to stop now. Instead, he ordered Bill to take the riding crop from him and to give me ten more hard whacks. I cried louder and shook more violently in fear when Bill let go of me. Master Jeff took his place holding my arms, keeping me steady on the chair…but he didn't suck my nipples.

"Get started!!" he yelled at Bill.

Bill ran the tip of the riding crop over my wounded ass cheeks. I could tell he was hesitating. He was not half as sadistic as Master Jeff was.

"Master Jeff, look at his ass cheeks…" Bill said imploringly to Master Jeff. "They're so red…"

"And they're going to be even more red when you're done whacking him ten more times," Master Jeff said to Bill. "Bill, he came here for this. It was his choice to be worked over this way. *Now, get started…*"

As Master Jeff spoke harshly to Bill I cringed in the chair, shaking like a leaf, and cried pitifully. Master Jeff was right. I had brought this all on myself. Stupid me, I didn't realize just how much I was getting into. Then, my thoughts were cut short when Bill brought the riding crop down on my ass cheeks.

"OWWWWW!!!" I roared.

"That's it Bill, give it to him good!" Master Jeff said encouragingly and Bill whacked me a second time.

"AAAAYYRRR!!!" I seethed through clenched teeth.

Master Jeff held me tightly by my arms, keeping me steady on the chair as Bill whacked me a third and fourth time. I was shaking and trembling so fiercely that Master Jeff had to hold me tighter and tighter in place.

"Please Bill…" I croaked.

Bill whacked me a fifth time, a sixth time, and I cried and screamed louder and louder. I leaned my head down, sweating like crazy as Bill gave me the seventh whack. By now my blindfold was soaked in tears. Bill whacked me an eight and ninth time. I screamed in agony through clenched teeth. Mucous dripped from my nostrils, onto my trembling lips and into my mouth, totally revolting.

"Okay Bill, for the last one give it to him really fucking hard," Master Jeff ordered.

Bill did as he was told and when I received the tenth and hardest whack yet my head snapped straight up and I let out a horrible wail of pain. Bill dropped the riding crop on the floor as Master Jeff untied my wrists from the chair…

A few moments later I was sitting on the couch with Bill. He was holding me in his arms, soothing me, kissing my face and stroking my sweat sopped hair as I cried and shook like a baby. The blindfold was off me and Bill was using it to wipe my tears from my face.

"Easy, easy…" Bill said and crossed a leg on his knee, knowing what I wanted.

Master Jeff sat nearby in the chair watching the spectacle in front of him. I leaned forward, placed a trembling hand on Bill's socked calf and he kissed the top of my head.

"Getting everything you came here for?" Master Jeff asked me mockingly. "I really hope you are because we're working hard for you…"

I looked over at him with anger showing in my eyes.

"*I'm speechless…*" I whispered through my tears.

After a while I stopped crying and boldly took a few sucks off one of Bill's big nipples. He moaned contentedly. A few minutes later I was sitting in between Master Jeff and Bill on the couch. Master Jeff was squeezing one of my nipples as Bill stroked my hard cock which was now sticking out of the fly opening in my briefs. I was throbbing like crazy and so glad to have Bill jacking me off at last. He held my juicy balls in his other hand and gently squeezed them as he stroked me more and more.

"Goin' to shoot a big fucking load…" Bill whispered and licked my earlobe. "You always shoot such big creamy loads…"

Master Jeff squeezed and twisted the fuck out of my nipple and Bill stroked me faster and faster.

"OHHHHHH yeah, getting fucking close now you fuckers…" I grunted breathlessly.

Then, I shot my load, cumming like crazy, shooting gobs and gobs of hot creamy sperm all over my chest.

"ARRRRRRRHHHH!!! YEAH, fucking A!" I roared in ecstasy. "MOTHERFUCKIN' A you guys!"

My cum splattered and landed all over my chest, my nipples and dripped onto my stomach area. Bill held my cock tightly, a look of awe in his eyes as I shot more and more creamy jazz. Finally, I was done, and Bill let go of my manhood. Master Jeff stopped squeezing my nipple and I leaned back on the couch, catching my breath.

"Feeling good?" Master Jeff asked me and kissed me gently on the cheek as Bill ran his tongue through the globs of cum all over me, lapping it up.

"Oh yes Master Jeff, I'm feeling real fucking great now..." I said to him, smiling.

He kissed me again on the cheek. Bill slurped my cum off my nipples and I shuddered on the couch. I'm always real sensitive after shooting a big pent-up load, especially around my nipples.

"Okay Bill, lick up as much of that cream of his as possible and then we'll get ready for round two of working him over..." Master Jeff said with authority in his voice.

"Round two???" I asked in a high pitched tone of voice.

"Sure," Master Jeff said and squeezed one of my nipples hard and painfully. "You didn't think we were done did you?"

My smile dropped from my face in an instant.

"Fuck..." I whispered. *"Oh fuck, fuck, fuck..."*

Now granted I was untied at that moment and could have simply gotten dressed and walked out of there. But, as indicated already, I am a man of my word and I knew I would see this through to the ghastly end... So, about fifteen minutes later I was sitting on the chair with my arms at my sides and my feet together. Master Jeff and Bill were having a grand old time tying me securely to the chair, winding rope over and over my upper body. My feet were already tied together rather securely. I sat there helplessly in my white briefs, white sweat socks and construction boots as the two men made sport of tying me up good and fucking tight. I was feeling so wasted and beaten to shit at that moment. They had really worked me over so much already. And now I was in for what Master Jeff called round two. At least they weren't going to whack my ass at the moment. The way I was seated they could not possibly get to it. Even sitting was painful however on my wounded ass cheeks. When they were done tying me tightly to the chair Master Jeff stepped behind me and ran his fingers through my hair.

"Comfortable?" he asked me mockingly.

"Yeah, real comfy," I replied sarcastically.

Master Jeff ran his hands over my shoulders and down to my chest. He gave my exposed nipples a good hard squeeze and twist each.

"OWWWW!!!" I bellowed.

Bill stood in front of me, looking hungrily at the bulge in my briefs. Yeah, unbelievably I was hard as a fucking rock, even after having shot a hefty load.

"Okay Bill, let's get started..." Master Jeff said and stepped over to the couch.

He reached under the couch and brought out two old worn leather belts. He handed one to Bill and they stood a few feet away from me on the sides of the chair I was tied to.

"WH-what now???" I asked, fear coursing through me like wildfire.

Master Jeff smiled, swung the belt and the leather connected with my thigh closest to him.

"OWWWWWW!!!" I screamed in a man's pain.

Without being told to Bill swung his belt at my other thigh and whacked it hard.

"OWWWWWW you fuckers!!" I ranted as they swung their belts together, whacking my thighs harder and harder with each blow.

"Man, he's going to be real wounded when we send him home later..." Master Jeff mused and whacked my thigh again and again.

I clenched my teeth, closed my eyes real tight and hung my head back as the two men beat my thighs relentlessly with the leather belts.

"I wonder how he's going to explain all the marks on his body to that lover of his when he gets home..." Master Jeff laughed meanly.

As I thought about being at home with my lover my eyes filled with new tears and they streamed freely out of my closed eyelids, soaking my face anew.

"Bastards!!" I cried loudly over and over. "Fucking sadists!"

They whacked my thighs so much and so hard I thought for sure they were going to make me bleed. But above all other things Master Jeff is a careful sadist. After a few final whacks he ordered Bill to stop whacking me. They stopped beating me with the leather belts, put the belts down on the couch and stood over me, watching me shake, tremble and cry while tied to the chair.

"I swear to God I never thought I would see the day when I would have *you* here like this," Master Jeff said and ran his fingers over my chin.

I looked up at him through my tear filled eyes and for an instant he smiled lovingly at me. The thin line between sadism and romance had been briefly crossed it seemed.

"Bill, get the aloe cream that's in the bathroom," Master Jeff said, still looking at me and stroking my chin. "I want you to soothe him."

A few minutes later I was standing, staring straight ahead. My hands were cuffed behind me again and now my briefs were completely off me. My cock was semi hard as Bill knelt in front of me smearing the aloe cream over my ass cheeks and thighs, soothing my tortured parts. A few times Bill gave my wounded ass cheeks a gentle squeeze as he applied the cream to them. Master Jeff sat on the couch supervising Bill.

"OHHHHH, that feels nice…" I crooned as Bill's fingers massaged the cream against my ass cheeks some more.

With a smug look on his face Bill pushed a greasy finger into my asshole and twisted it around in there a few times.

"OHHHHH!!!" I cried out and almost jumped out of my boots.

Bill prodded my hole for a few good seconds and then yanked his finger out. Already my cock was hard. Bill squeezed more of the cream into his hands and massaged it over my reddened thighs.

"MMMM…" I said softly and smiled sheepishly.

Then, Bill put the tube of lotion down on the floor and looked over at Master Jeff. Master Jeff smiled and nodded. Bill smiled, and then with a greasy hand he grabbed my hard cock.

"OHHHHH yeah!!" I roared and gyrated my hips seductively as Bill began stroking my cock slowly. "OHHHHH fuck, FUCK that feels so good man!! Damn, I love you guys!!"

Master Jeff stepped behind me, reached around me with both hands, and squeezed my nipples gently as Bill stroked me more and more.

"OHHHH fuck yeah…" I crooned.

Master Jeff kissed the back of my neck and licked my earlobes as he squeezed my nipples harder and harder.

"OH FUCK yeah, goin' to make me shoot a second fucking load of cream…" I moaned.

Goose bumps broke out all over my body as the two men stroked and squeezed me into ecstasy. A short while later I felt myself about to cum a second time that afternoon.

"OHHHHHH yeah, yeah!!" I roared as I shot my load in Bill's hand.

"Another giant load of cream," Bill exclaimed in awe.

As my cum filled his hands he lapped it up like a hungry puppy. I shook and shuddered in wild ecstasy as I came and came. When I was done Master Jeff let go of my nipples and Bill stood up straight. Master

Jeff grabbed my arms, turned me around facing him, and gathered me into his strong arms. He kissed me gently on the side of my neck over and over again, stroking the back of my neck at the same time. Chills coursed through me at his touch and kisses as I was feeling real sensitive and sexy after having just shot that second load.

"You're doing well…" Master Jeff whispered in my ear and kissed my neck again.

Then, a few minutes passed and I found myself standing in the archway of Master Jeff's living room. My wrists were roped above me to a hook that was secured in the ceiling, and I was blindfolded again.

"Still love us?" Master Jeff asked me mockingly and ran a finger over my left, very exposed, sweaty armpit.

Bill was already lapping at my right armpit. Actually, it was Bill's idea to have tied me up that way so that my armpits would be exposed for his sleazy licking pleasure.

"Yeah, I love you both," I replied and Master Jeff whacked my ass hard with the leather paddle.

"OWWWWWWW!!!" I yelled in pain.

Then, Master Jeff whacked my ass again and again, harder and harder with each blow as Bill sucked painfully at my armpit.

"AARRRHHHH!!!" I cried out and writhed in both pain and pleasure. "FUCKERS!!"

Master Jeff chuckled and whacked my ass over and over again. I was beginning to wonder when it would be all over but the afternoon was still kind of young and Master Jeff had waited a long time for this. I knew he wasn't going to let up on me anytime soon. I began crying again as he whacked me harder and harder with the leather paddle. I actually found myself wishing they had tied my feet together. At least that way I would be safely balanced in place. But I think Master Jeff was enjoying seeing me dance around and around in pain, blindfolded and looking helpless in my bondage. I screamed in pain and moaned in ecstasy as Bill lapped my armpits and Master Jeff whacked my poor ass over and over. I clenched my teeth and seethed in pain.

"I'm goin' to need more of that damned cream rubbed on my ass Bill!!" I yelled. "OWWWWWW!!!"

"Sure thing, after you've licked my sweaty socked feet again," Bill said and kissed my armpits a few times each.

Now that was something to look forward to…

Finally, Master Jeff stopped paddling my ass cheeks.

"That was twenty hard ones you little bastard…" Master Jeff whispered in my ear.

If my calculating was correct that now made a total of one hundred whacks I had suffered to my ass cheeks. Not to mention the beating they had given my thighs earlier. Bill continued licking my armpits and then I felt it…I could not believe it was happening. Master Jeff roughly pushed my reddened and wounded ass cheeks apart and began to slowly push his hard cock into my hole.

"OHHHHHH shit…*ooohhhh fuck…ohhhh yeah…*" I moaned loudly. "Goin' to fuck me…he's goin' to plow my damned asshole…"

Bill held me by my hips and went right on lapping my armpits as Master Jeff plunged his meat stick into my hole.

"OHHHHHH yeah!!" Master Jeff roared and began thrusting in me…hard.

My cock was hard and throbbing in front of me, swinging back and forth as I bucked around in my bondage. GAWD, I was beyond ecstasy and pain at that moment. The two men had taken me past both thresholds. With Master Jeff fucking me and Bill licking my armpits I felt like I was floating on air. Master Jeff fucked me with brute force, thrusting harder and harder into my most private crevice. Bill sucked my armpits and squeezed my nipples a few times.

"Driving me wild…" I whispered breathlessly. *"Driving me fucking wild…"*

When Master Jeff shot his load he spewed a giant man-sized load into me. One of his loads equaled three of my big loads.

"OHHHHHHHH YEAH!!" Master Jeff cried out and threw his arms around me as he shot his load into my hole.

He hugged me tight and held me so close to himself while he shot his load that I thought I would suffocate.

"OHHHH fuck…" Master Jeff panted and kissed the back of my neck a few times. "Fucking sweet hole you have…"

Finally, Master Jeff's cock slid out of my hole and he took the blindfold off me. I was gasping for breath as he stepped in front of me next to Bill. They both stood there looking me over. Master Jeff casually packed his cock back into his pants.

"He looks so hot all tied like that eh Bill?" Master Jeff asked.

"He sure does," Bill replied, rubbing the hard-on he was sporting in his boxer briefs.

Slowly, Bill stepped behind me, pulling his boner out of the front of his boxer briefs.

"Oh shit, here we go again..." I whispered, knowing Bill was about to fuck me too.

Bill positioned himself behind me, pushed my ass cheeks apart and slowly pushed his huge Irish cock into me.

"OHHHHHHH GAWD, you fucking guys..." I moaned.

Bill's cock felt like it was nibbling at my moist opening as it slid in deeper with each passing second. Master Jeff squeezed my (by now sore) nipples and twisted them in his fingers as Bill plunged his cock deep inside me.

"OHHHHH yeah, yeah," Bill whispered breathlessly.

He stood with his hands clenched into fists at his sides as his cock slid in and out of my bunghole. Bill, like Master Jeff fucked me hard. My cock was still rage hard in front of me...waiting to shoot a third load. But I would have to endure more erotic torture before I would be allowed that pleasure. As Bill shot his load into my hole Master Jeff pinched and twisted my nipples hard.

"OHHHHH FUCK!!!" I roared in pain as Bill moaned and groaned in a man's passion behind me.

When Bill was done his cock slowly slid out of my hole and he stepped back in front of me with Master Jeff.

"Feeling good?" Master Jeff asked Bill.

"Feeling great," Bill replied.

"Good, let's work our boy some more..." Master Jeff said with an evil grin.

I leaned my head back between my arms and closed my eyes in fear as Master Jeff walked to his bedroom, leaving Bill and I alone for a moment. When I felt Bill's hand on my chest I opened my eyes, leaned my head forward and looked at him.

"What the hell does he have in mind for me now???" I asked Bill desperately.

"I honestly don't know," Bills said as he ran his hands over my hips, his big cock still sticking out of his boxer briefs. "God almighty but you do look good all tied up and helpless like this..."

He pulled me close to himself and clamped his mouth down on mine...kissing me hard on the lips. My cock swelled even more in front of me.

"Well, well, now isn't this sweet?" Master Jeff said from behind as he walked back into the living room.

Bill stopped kissing me, turned and looked at Master Jeff. Master Jeff was holding an ankle bar in his hands as he stepped over to us. He handed it to Bill.

"Get this thing on his ankles," Master Jeff said sternly to Bill and then looked at me. "And get those feet of yours spread apart... NOW!!!"

I did as I was told and moments later the ankle bar was on me, keeping my feet spread good and wide, just as Master Jeff wanted them to be. My cock was now pointing straight up, hard and throbbing and oozing pre cum, my balls hanging low in my hairy sac, (just the way Master Jeff wanted them as well) and my ass cheeks were spread apart, revealing my still somewhat moist hole. I stood there helplessly as the two men squeezed my nipples hard and ran their hands over and over my body.

"OHHHHH man..." I moaned helplessly. "What's the point of this???"

"Well I'll tell you Shit-head," Master Jeff replied, reaching into his pants pocket. "Seeing as you're so damned anxious to know..."

Master Jeff took two metal ball bearings out of his pocket which were attached to long strings. He held them up for Bill and me to see.

"*Oh shit...*" I whispered.

Master Jeff closed his hand in a fist. Then, he and Bill squatted in front of me and began tonguing my balls... hard.

Now, most guys I know (and I'm sure you will agree with me) love to have their balls tongued. I don't. For some reason I find it to be very painful and annoying. I suppose it can be said that I have super sensitive balls. I had made the mistake of telling Master Jeff and Bill this one time in the past... and they were now taking full advantage of it.

"MMMMM..." Master Jeff crooned as his tongue slid over my ball that he was working on next to Bill. "Let's really apply the pressure to these big gonads of his. When they're good and swollen we'll tie the ball bearings onto them. Then we'll really see the little bastard cry and squirm. They really weigh those ball bearings..."

The two men each pulled one of my testicles into their mouth and ran their mangy tongues over them, applying as much pressure to them as possible. I was already crying and squirming in pain. A few minutes went by and then they took my balls out of their mouths... and went on tonguing them.

"Damn, my poor aching balls..." I seethed.

"By the time we're done torturing these nuts of yours you won't want to shoot a load for a week Hot shot," Master Jeff said tauntingly.

"AAARRRHHH you fuckers!!" I roared in absolute agony.

When they finally stopped tonguing my balls my most private of parts were all swollen and throbbing miserably. I had never felt such pain before.

"*G-guys, please...*" I begged as Master Jeff handed Bill one of the ball bearings.

Ignoring me they proceeded to tie the strings attached to the ball bearings slowly and tightly around my swollen and aching gonads.

"AAAAYYYYY..." I cried out awfully, tears streaming down my face.

I rocked back and forth on my boot heels. With that ankle bar on my feet it was the only movement I could possibly manage. My arms were numb at this point from being tied above me for so long. I was sweating profusely and my cock was achingly hard, if you can believe that that is. My tears stained my face and mucous continued dripping from my nose and onto my trembling lips. The pain in my balls was immense as my two buddies finished tying off the strings around them. They then held the ball bearings in their hands...ready to let go of them at Master Jeff's order.

"Okay Bill, when I say so let go of the ball bearing," Master Jeff said. "It should just about reach the floor. The pain he's going to feel when these ball bearings tug on his balls is going to make the spankings we gave him seem light..."

"Guys, no...no..." I pleaded through clenched teeth. "God, oh God, this is too much..."

"Okay Bill, now..." Master Jeff said and they let go of the ball bearings.

What happened next seemed to happen in slow motion. They let go of the ball bearings. The ball bearings dropped toward the floor. And pain shot through me like I had never felt before. For a second I thought my balls had been ripped off my body.

"AAYYYYRRRRR!!!" I roared in complete and utter agony.

The ball bearings sure did weigh. The way they were pulling on my balls was beyond anything I had ever felt before. The room spun in front of me, I was in a sort of stupor, and I could have sworn that Master Jeff and Bill were taking turns kissing me on the mouth. Actually *they were* taking turns kissing me on the mouth, forcing their tongues into my mouth and sucking my tongue. When they stopped kissing me they squatted back down by my poor wounded balls. They each gave my balls a few hard licks and I cried more and more in pain.

"Want to jack him off?" Master Jeff asked Bill. "Do that and he'll really scream..."

"He looks like he's going to pass out," Bill responded, sounding truly concerned now. "Maybe we should untie him and give him a break..."

Master Jeff ran a hand over one of my thighs and looked up at me. My head was lolling back and forth and my eyes were half closed. Master Jeff looked (for maybe a second) like he felt sorry for me.

"Okay, but only a short break..." Master Jeff said sternly. "He still has a lot more to endure before the afternoon is over..."

They untied the ball bearings from my balls, took the ankle bar off my feet and untied my wrists. When my arms fell at my sides the two men held me upright and walked me over to the couch. Bill sat down on the couch with me in his arms. Master Jeff went to the kitchen to get me some very much needed water. Bill held me tightly against himself and kissed the top of my head as I shook and cried.

"B-Bill..." I whispered hoarsely.

"Shhh..." Bill said and kissed me again.

"*Bill, I had no idea...*" I whispered and closed my eyes.

Bill stroked my hair and whispered "I love you" in my ear. At that moment Master Jeff returned to the living room with a bottle of cool mineral water. I leaned forward on the couch as he handed me the bottle.

"You all right?" Master Jeff asked me and squatted down in front of me as I sipped the water.

I nodded that I was okay. Then, I leaned closer to Master Jeff and kissed his lips once.

"He really is something," Master Jeff said to Bill as I drank more of the water.

About fifteen minutes later I was feeling somewhat better...but not for long as I was about to find out. I was standing in the center of the living room as Master Jeff and Bill laid a long metal weight bar across my shoulders. They ordered me to place my wrists over it. I did as I was told and they proceeded to tie my wrists securely to the bar, fastening it to my shoulders.

"What the hell is this all about?" I asked them angrily.

"Looks like that break we gave him made him cocky all over again," Master Jeff said to Bill. "Well, what we're going to do now should cure that real quick…"

When the bar was securely tied onto my shoulders Master Jeff and Bill both placed twenty pound round weights on the sides of it.

"OHHHH shit…" I grunted and tried my best to hold the weight on my shoulders.

As my knees almost gave out Master Jeff whacked my backside hard with the back of his hand.

"OWWWWWWW!!!" I cried out and straightened up.

"Walk Asshole!" Master Jeff yelled at me. "To the archway and back…"

Looking at him in disbelief I clenched my teeth and walked toward the archway where they had tortured my balls. When I reached the archway I slowly turned and walked back to my two buddies.

"Again!!" Master Jeff ordered.

"*Shit…*" I whispered, not feeling cocky at all anymore.

I walked to the archway again, the weight across my shoulders feeling like it was weighing more and more with each step I took. In no time I was sweating all over again. I made my way slowly back over to the two men…where they were waiting with more weights.

"Oh no, no, noooo…" I whimpered as they each placed ten pound weights on the bar.

"That's sixty pounds plus the bar Asshole," Master Jeff said and squeezed my swollen balls.

"AAAHHRR!!!" I cried loudly and almost buckled.

"Walk, NOW!!" Master Jeff hollered.

I hung my head down and walked again toward the archway. I was sniveling like a child. Halfway to the archway I thought I was going to pass out for sure. I stopped walking and took very deep breaths.

"He can't move…" Bill said, sounding alarmed.

"This will get him moving," Master Jeff said and picked up the riding crop.

He stomped behind me and whacked me hard across the ass with it.

"AYYYYRRR!!!" I screamed and my head snapped up.

I walked to the archway and turned around. I saw that Master Jeff and Bill were waiting with more weights to put on the bar. I hung my head down and walked miserably back over to them.

"Man, he looks real shitty," Master Jeff said as I stood before him and Bill. "What do you think Hot shot; can you handle another twenty pounds on that bar?"

"N-n-no..." I said breathlessly, my tears soaking my face. "No Master Jeff..."

Master Jeff smiled triumphantly and then he ordered Bill to help him get the bar off my shoulders.

"Thank you, *thank you, thank you,"* I panted over and over.

Moments later I was on my knees in front of my two masters. I leaned down, kissed Master Jeff's boots numerous times and then kissed Bill's loafers and socks. I was beaten to shit and didn't think I could take anymore. I kissed Bill's socks up and down, savoring the funky odor of his foot sweat as it invaded my nostrils. I ran my tongue over Master Jeff's boots, polishing them with my saliva. My cock was hard as a rock and throbbing. I knew that soon Master Jeff would want for me to shoot my load. The way they had tortured my balls it was sure to hurt when I shot my third load and that's what this was all about...a test of my strength and endurance...it was all about me hurting.

"Did you ever think you'd see the day when this shit head would be kneeling before you Bill?" Master Jeff asked Bill.

"No, I still find it hard to believe..." Bill replied.

"Shows what a little discipline will do," Master Jeff said. "Okay Hot shot things are really going to heat up for you now..."

With that Master Jeff reached down, grabbed a handful of my hair and yanked me meanly to my feet.

"YOWWWWW!!!" I cried out in pain as he hauled me up by my hair.

I stood between the two men as they squeezed my nipples, rubbed my chest and pinched my red ass cheeks.

"Oh man are you in for it now Hot shot..." Master Jeff whispered menacingly in my ear.

I cringed in fear as they grabbed my arms tightly and pulled them behind me.

"Let's take him to the bedroom for the big finale..." Master Jeff stated authoritatively.

They hoisted me up a few inches off the floor and half walked, half carried me to the bedroom. In the bedroom Master Jeff made me take off my construction boots and socks. I was totally naked now. Next, he ordered me to climb on top of a large table that had been set up next to the bed. He said that I was to be atop the table on my hands and knees. Bill pulled my wrists together in front of me and quickly roped them tightly as Master Jeff stood behind me, taking in the sight of my red ass. He had pulled my hard cock out from between the backs of my thighs along with my still aching balls. I cringed in fear as Master Jeff tied my feet together followed by my knees and thighs, trapping my cock and balls behind my thighs.

"WH-what is all this for?" I asked Bill as he finished tying my wrists.

"You're going to find out," Bill said, sounding sad.

I looked around as Master Jeff walked over to his night table and took two tubes of Ben gay out of his underwear drawer.

"Like I said Hot shot, things are really going to heat up for you now," Master Jeff said as he stepped back over to me.

When I realized what I was in for now I looked at Bill desperately, my lips quivering.

"B-Bill…oh good God no…" I said hoarsely.

Bill just looked at me sadly and walked over to Master Jeff. Master Jeff handed Bill one of the tubes of Ben gay. Both men were now standing on opposite sides of the table, right next to my raised ass. Master Jeff gave my very red ass cheeks a few hard slaps.

"Okay Bill, squeeze some of that shit onto your fingers and then stick your slicked fingers up his ass," Master Jeff said in a commanding tone of voice. "Now we're really going to hear him yelp."

As Bill squeezed a good amount of the Ben gay onto his fingers Master Jeff gave my ass cheeks a few more hard slaps.

"OWWWW!!!" I cried in pain.

I turned my head, looking at the two men.

"Guys please," I said, tears already forming in my eyes.

But then, Bill's hand moved toward my ass and he inserted two of his Ben gay slicked fingers into my rectal hole. It didn't burn that much at first…it started to burn as he prodded my hole with his fingers.

"OHHHHHH fuck!!" I roared and hung my head down. *"Mother fuck!!! AAARRRHHH!! GOD!!!!!"*

As Bill worked the cream deeply into my hole Master Jeff continued slapping my ass cheeks…hard.

"OHHHHHHH NO, no!!!" I screeched now.

Tears flowed from my eyes and landed on top of the table I was on. I was sweating from fear and from the heat of the Ben gay in my slopped up asshole. I squirmed and thrashed miserably atop the table. Master Jeff opened his tube of Ben gay and smeared a good amount of it over my already red and burning ass cheeks. I cried miserably and in searing pain as he massaged the cream against my skin. Bill continued prodding my hole and I continued crying and squirming atop the table. I pressed my tear soaked face against my bound hands and cried profusely as my two buddies tortured my hole and ass cheeks with the Ben gay. Then, after a good while they stopped and stood at the sides of the table and watched me sweat and cry as the Ben gay continued to cook and torture me.

"Y-you bastards!!" I cried, raising my head off the table. *"F-fucking torturers!!!"*

I saw Master Jeff gesture to Bill and Bill stepped behind me. I expected him to rub more of the Ben gay into my hole but instead he leaned forward, grabbed my thighs and slurped my soft shriveled cock into his mouth. He sucked me slowly and lovingly to a new hard-on. Master Jeff stepped in front of me, cupped my chin in his hand and looked down at me.

"I love you more than you'll ever imagine," he said to me, leaned down and kissed my trembling lips.

As Master Jeff kissed me I shot my third load, right into Bill's mouth. He continued sucking me till every drop of my splooge was squeezed out...driving me wild. I roared in a wild man's passion and pain at the same time. When I was done squirting my two friends untied me and I hopped down off the table. They held me between themselves, taking turns kissing my lips, my cheeks, my neck and my face. I held onto them, still crying, but at the same time glad that it was over. I had proved myself worthy of their fantasies and worthy of myself when it came to my endurance levels. I had more than explored my submissive side and passed my own test. I was grateful to Master Jeff and Bill... believe it or not.

A while later after I had showered (a long shower I might add) we were all sitting on the couch. I was in between my two buddies, fully dressed. Master Jeff was still dressed as he had been earlier but Bill had put on his jeans, sneakers and a pull-over shirt.

"Are you okay?" Master Jeff asked me, looking at me like he was quite concerned.

"Yeah, I'm okay," I replied with a smile. "Nothing that won't heal..."

"I hope you don't hate us all that much..." Bill said with a smile on his face.

I threw my arms around Bill and said, "Never, I could never in a million years hate either of you..."

A short while later we sent out for Chinese food and beer and spent the remainder of the day like the buddies we are and always will be...

BIG GUY HAYNES OR IN THE CONTROL OF MEN

Oh man what a *fucked* up predicament I was in. And it was my own entire fault at that I might add, because *I* had foolishly agreed to let those two so-called buddies of mine have their way with me. *I* had agreed, knowing that in return I would have my big size fourteen feet serviced every which way possible. (Nothing gets me harder or more in motion than having my huge feet serviced bud.) I didn't realize when I had agreed to their conditions that I would be stretched out on my ripped and muscular back on a cushioned massage table (all six feet five inches of rock hard muscular me) strapped down good and fucking tight no less. And wearing just my calf length (left over from the long workday) smelly black nylon dress socks...*in a damned overheated steam room in the basement of the gym Alex and Ronald now owned.* (Y'all remember Alex and Ronald right? The worst, most sadistic practical jokers ever to grace God's green earth. Who can forget them? They're also the owner of the sleazy gay bar "The Local", the bar where United States sailor Private Higgins found himself tied to a stall door in the men's room with his cock and balls sticking out of a glory hole. FUCK, but that poor sailor had fallen for the trickery of Alex and Ronald and their bartender and once his cock and balls were tied off in that glory hole every cock hungry patron of that bar got a good sampling taste of the succulent sailor boy. I often wonder where he is now...) Fuckers that those two so called buddies of mine, Alex and Ronald could be. They hadn't mentioned strapping me down to the table when we had first talked about me lying in there and being serviced and made to shoot my load over and over. (Yeah and so much for that as well. The way I had been forcibly juiced I must have had a gallon of creamy executive jazz stored up in me by then.) But fuck it all you guys, what a sight I made, WHAT A FUCKING SIGHT, my muscular well-toned black body strapped down tight, atop that table, all nine goddamned succulent inches of my huge horse-sized cock pointing straight up at the ceiling as I lay there sweating. Sweating miserably and being feasted upon by Alex and Ronald's friends. (Take it from me you guys, there's something real kinky and explosive for a muscular guy like me, all strapped up and trapped, not being able to defend himself.) Zounds, and HELL, but those fuckers were literally cooking me in that steam room, in more ways than one I might add. Fuck, *all* those guys loved my huge hoof-like feet most of all. At size fourteen and still in my musty scented black socks from the workday who wouldn't love them? For feet fetishists of that caliber there's something real HOT and inviting about a tied up guy with giant feet wearing his black nylon dress socks. Those thin stinkers really outline the shape of a guy's feet in a real erotic light let me tell you. Each time a few new guys entered the steam room it was my damned feet they went after, per instructions of course. They also went after my big man-sized tits; tits so big a woman would be envious of them let me tell you, nice big suckable nubbies I got bud! Fuck, you could spend hours upon hours working on my damned man-sized tits and not get tired of them. DAMN, they're big and meaty to start with, but after slurping and tonguing them for a good long while they could actually be sucked like they were miniature sized cocks. I honestly think that if my man-sized tits are worked enough you'll get thick creamy milk from them, HAR, HAR, HAR!!! Fucking guys in that steam room sucked my big fat beefy tits like crazy, CRAZIER THAN CRAZY AT THAT, keeping my horse-sized cock good and fucking hard and oozing and oozing pre cum. It was only after those two jokers had gotten me into the position that I'm describing to you that I found out their friends could play with and use any part of my body, *except my damned horse cock.* I was suffering madly and nearly insanely from what I learned is called cum depravation. Never before had I known what the fuck that is, seeing as I always got my way where shooting my load was concerned. Feeding me that potent aphrodisiac, juicing me as I call it, (through my asshole no less JEEZ) only added to my horny and wretched misery. That was really fucked up let me tell you, them feeding me that slop through my damned asshole. The conditions also allowed Alex and Ronald to keep me in that steam room for as long as they chose to. And from all points I wasn't getting out any time soon. You see, upstairs in the "Closed to the General Public" gym Alex and Ronald were having a "Grand Opening Celebration" for their new state of the art exercise establishment. They had invited a mess of their friends (no doubt some of the patrons of the sleazy bar "The Local") to come and share in the festivities, including yours truly, Haynes, Big guy Haynes as my friends call me. Unfortunately for me I had become the star attraction at the party, I was the goddamned meat market, the party favor so to speak…

"OOOOOHHH yeah, SHHEEETTT, fucking guys're driving me crazy here," I croaked throatily in the steam and heat filled room as four of Alex and Ronald's buddies feasted on me like I was a buffet at a party, which from all points at the moment *I really was.*

My body was sopped in sweat from head to toe (and glistening in all my musculature I might add) as two of the guys sucked and slurped heartily on my big fat tits and the other two leaned over my smelly black socked feet, licking, kissing and sucking them. They held me by the calves, caressing my legs as they sucked crazily at my stinking socked toes.

"OHHHH yeah, go for it you foot freaks," I whispered through my sweaty and trembling thick lips. "Fuckers, I may be the guy all strapped up and in just my damned socks for your pleasure, but *you have to do as I say.* Those are the rules and I say suck my goddamned feet and eat my big tits!"

My horse cock was pulsing madly and huge between my muscular thighs and my big fat bulging balls rested atop that cushioned table, aching for release. Release that I knew they weren't going to get any time soon.

"Those are the rules eh Big guy Haynes?" one of the guys at my feet asked me, looking at me across my massively muscular strapped down body through the clouds of steam. "The rules also dictate that you DON'T get out of this sweat box till Alex and Ronald say so."

He leaned down and flicked his tongue over my socked toes.

"And Alex and Ronald aren't saying so, not for a long while you oversized stud," the guy chuckled and slurped his mangy tongue across the bottom of my foot. "So tell me, *just who is giving the orders around here?*" The sounds of chuckling, slurping and panting filled the over heated steam room as the four guys went to town on me. After a while they switched places and the guys who had been at my tits went down to my feet and vice versa.

"Yeah, everybody gets to sample my good parts eh guys?" I asked them, lifting my head up off the table. "How about some water?"

One of the guys on my tits automatically stopped what he was doing and dashed out of the steam room to get one of many bottles of mineral water. While he was temporarily off my nipple his friend kept it occupied by swirling it in his thumb and fingers while sucking and slurping the other one.

"OHHHHH SHHHEEETT, yeah, feels so fucking good you guys," I panted.

The rules of this mess I was in also dictated that I had to be given water every few minutes or whenever I asked for it. I was also not to be under any circumstances left alone for any length of time, no matter how short. Obviously that meant I would be feasted on constantly during the party, *constantly* and to the point when I would eventually be begging to be let to shoot my damned load. But being that I was the party favor my need to shoot my load was unimportant. What these guys cared about was getting *their* rocks off. The guy who had stepped out of the steam room to get me some water returned with a quart-sized bottle of mineral water.

"Down the hatch Big guy," he said, placing a hand behind my head and in my long sweat soaked dreadlocks and placing the tip of the bottle to my lips.

I slowly sipped the water, knowing that if I gulped it down too fast I could cause myself some serious cramps. As I was sucked, slurped and feasted upon I drank the water. It was delicious to say the least.

"Man oh man, just look at his lips wrapped around that bottle, fucking beautiful big lips you got Big guy Haynes," the guy feeding me the water said in awe and kissed me on the cheek.

I drank down more than half of the bottle of water. The rest of it the guy spilled onto my big chest and pecs before resuming sucking and slurping my big tit.

"OHHHHH yeah, feeling real fucking good now you bastards," I panted as my feet and tits were serviced and worked on with real and utter gusto. "That water cooled me down real nice..."

When the four guys couldn't take the heat anymore they took their cocks in hand and began stroking themselves, their cocks aimed at me.

"OHHHH yeah, fuckers're making me real fucking jealous here," I grunted madly, looking at my big hard horse cock through the clouds of steam. "Man, someone stroke me just a few times, that's all I ask you bastards!"

My huge horse cock oozed and oozed more and more pre cum. It slid down the sides of my erection, driving me further into a frenzy. Watching as my buddies stroked themselves and at times each other was making me batty. Having had my tits and feet serviced so much had me in a total lather as it was. My big horse cock glistened with my pre cum, long, beefy and hard with sweat as well which also slid down the sides of my pulsing shaft. My cock (as I will refer to it from here on out) twitched back and forth, practically painfully hard between my muscular thighs. My sweaty and stinking balls ached for release.

"OHHH yeah, I'm getting close already you guys," the guy who had fed me the water blurted in the heat. "Fucking sucking Big guy Haynes' feet and tits has driven me insane. OHHHH yeah!!! FUCKING A you stud!!"

The guy shot his load all over my sweat sopped chest and stomach areas followed by two of his buddies who shot their creamy white boy loads all over my socked feet, my legs and upper body. The fourth guy, a sexy lanky blond number straddled me atop the table and slid his throbbing manhood into my mouth, filling my craw with his white chicken meat.

"HRRRRMMMFFF…" I gurgled as the guy held me by my ears, rocked my head up and down and shot his load down my throat, forcing me to eat his ball juice.

The sounds of men in passion and heat filled the steam room. The sounds of my scoffing down a white guy's cum filled the steam room as well. Cum spurted and flew all over me, the scent of it wafting through the steam room. When I was done eating the blond guy's cum he slid his cock out of my mouth, let go of my ears and climbed down off the table, panting breathlessly as he did so.

"Jeez, thanks for the appetizer guy," I said, smacking my cum crusted lips together.

Every time one of the guy's spurts splattered on me my cock grew harder and more potent. Pre cum oozed from my wide sexy slit nearly in torrents. Fuck, but I was more than jealous at that point. *I really needed to shoot my load.* You see I had been in that damned steam room for more than a few hours at that point. More than a few hours of being sucked, slurped on and eaten like a buffet. My socks were a mess of sweat and saliva and cum and my tits had been worked up to twice their normal size. And now I had even been made to eat white boy cum. (And where my tits are concerned that's saying something let me tell you, seeing as my tits are really big to begin with.) And I was hornier than a bitch in heat on a hot summer night. On the floor against the wall were mineral water bottles that I had drunk from, more than a few of them at that point. Some of them were filled with piss, *my piss*. Some of the guys had gulped down my piss before exiting the steam room after having had their fun with me. (That really did a number on me man, watching those perverts control my cock, watching them scoff down my piss from my big font, but expert enough to not let me shoot my load of cream.) But I wasn't to be made to shoot my damned load. *That* was going to be Alex and Ronald's pleasure and no one else's when the time came. After all four of the guys were done shooting their loads they caught their breath, even the guy who had made me suck his cock and eat his damned offering. They slowly exited the steam room, thanking me mockingly as they went, all of them naked as the day they had been born. I sarcastically told them they were welcome and balled my huge hands into meaty fists of frustration. *FUCK!!!* Strapped down tight and no fucking way of getting to my cock to give the big guy some relief. I wasn't alone for a minute. The door of the steam room opened and four more of Alex and Ronald's friends entered, one of them coming prepared with a bottle of mineral water.

"Hey Big guy Haynes, enjoying the party?" one of the guys asked me, taking one of my big feet in his hands.

"Y-yeah, great, just great, one of you clowns better feed me some water so you can empty that damned bottle," I replied. "You see, I have to piss...*again*..."

Chuckling, all four of the guys went to work on me, slurping at my stinking socked feet and big fat tits...

And here we go again I thought miserably and in ecstasy at the same time...

Before I go any further with all this let me tell you about me *and* about how I wound up in the predicament I am relating herein...

My name is Trevor Haynes, Big guy Haynes to my friends. I work as a corporate accounts manager for a bank located in mid-town Manhattan. I'm thirty-four years old. I'm African-American and damned proud of my heritage let me tell you. I stand six feet five inches tall and I'm muscular and well-toned from all the workouts I put myself through at the gym on a daily basis. Fucking built like a brick shit house to put it plainly. I don't think a day goes by that I don't workout good and fucking hard after work. I have brown hair styled into shoulder length dreadlocks and deep sexy brown eyes. My feet (as I told you) are all of size fourteen, triple E on less. Fuck, but its difficult to find shoes and socks in my size let me tell you. And between my tree-trunk like muscular legs I'm hung like a goddamned horse, all nine inches of beefy fat cock, more than a mouthful for anybody hungry for it that's for sure. I know that those fuckers feasting on me in the steam room that night had to wrestle with themselves not to go near my huge cock. But little did I know just how much I would be made to shoot my load that night as well. My well-hung testicles are just about the size of two golf balls, all succulent and furry. On the night I'm telling you about herein I had simply stopped by Alex and Ronald's gym to check the place out. During the week before they had called me to tell me that they were ready for their "Grand Opening Party" and invited me. Sitting at my desk I smiled from ear to ear, thanking them for the invitation but politely declining, citing the fact that I get up for work very early in the morning. I promised to make it up to them on a weekend by joining them for dinner. They would not hear of it. They suggested I just "*stop by*" then on my way home the night of the "Grand Opening" party, just so I could see the place. Still smiling I said that would be fine, adding that I would be there around six PM. Fuck, I had no idea that I would wind up spending the night and then some there. So, a week or so later on a Thursday night, dressed in a navy blue pin-striped suit, a white shirt, a silk patterned tie and black slip-on wingtips I left my office and took the train a few stops downtown to what was called "Alex and Ronald's Iron-Man Local Gym." I have to admit the place was impressive, all three floors of it. On the top floor were free weights, machines of every make and model for every body type and every body part and a small office for the gym staff. On the second floor were more cardio machines that I can tell you about. There were stair masters, treadmills, exercise bikes and off to the side a good sized aerobics studio. There were also two small offices on the cardio floor. We stopped in one of the offices to sit and have a health drink before continuing the tour down to the basement of the gym or should I say down to hell, down to what would be my hell.

"Well, I must say I am impressed with this place," I said to Alex and Ronald, sitting in front of the desk with one of my big feet resting on my knee. "You two have sure put as much work into putting this place together as you did with that bar you own."

Alex is a tall and lanky blond white guy with mischievous looking blue eyes. He's in his early thirties and I've always thought of him as a joker, a joker who enjoys playing mean tricks on unsuspecting guys... unsuspecting guys like me. Ronald is also pretty tall, but built more muscular than his good buddy Alex. He's almost my height with brown wavy hair and dark eyes. Like Alex he's in his early thirties. I always get the feeling that he and Alex were a little more than good buddies, owning a bar first and now a gym proved my theory correct. They were now business partners, the owners of two establishments.

"Not to mention a lot of money Big guy Haynes," Ronald said standing behind me and gently tugging on one of my sexy dreadlocks while Alex sat behind the desk facing me.

"Now tell us Trevor, how about *you* joining up right now?" Alex asked me as I took a sip of my health drink, apple flavored and real thick. "I have the paperwork right here in this desk. All you have to do is sign your name. We have more than a hundred members already."

"Well I'll tell you guys, it's a great place you've got here, no doubt," I began and sipped my drink again. "But I'm really satisfied with the membership I have at the gym I've been going to for some time now."

"Okay, I'll accept that for now," Alex said with a smile. "But when you do get tired of your old gym please let us know."

"You two will be the first to know, that I promise," I said and raised my glass in salute to my two buddies.

While my glass was raised Ronald picked up the pitcher of the apple flavored health drink and refilled my glass to the top.

"Hey thanks, but I don't think I'll be able to finish all this," I said and sipped the drink.

"Down the hatch Big guy Haynes, it'll put hair on your chest," Ronald chuckled.

"Ha, I got more hair on my chest and other places than I know what to do with," I replied with a grin.

"Okay, let's finish your tour," Alex piped up and stood behind the desk. "In the lowest level of the place we have the locker rooms, shower rooms, bathrooms, a swimming pool and a sauna and steam room."

"A steam room?" I asked as I got to my feet, my drink in hand. "Man that is one thing the gym that I go to doesn't have. I always wished they had a damned steam room."

"And our steam room is oversized with a big table in it," Ronald said, giving one of my upper arms a squeeze. "A table big enough for even a guy your size to relax comfortably on after a long grueling workout."

"Hmm, I get the feeling I'm still being coaxed into applying for a membership here," I said, taking a hearty sip of my drink.

"Well come on, lets go and see what there is to see and maybe *you will* change your mind," Alex said as we exited the office, me with my drink in hand.

We walked down the stairs to the lowest level and to put it truthfully the locker room was immaculate, with rugs on the floor and vents sucking in and blowing out fresh air. The swimming pool was Olympic sized and the sauna was enticing. But it was the steam room that impressed me most of all. Bedecked with benches done up in tiers on the sides and a long cushioned massage table right in the dead center of it, it was HUGE.

"Man, how much power does it take to steam this room up?" I asked, looking around the (at the moment) cool dimly lit steam room.

"A lot," Ronald said to me. "And believe me, it gets good and hot and steamy in here. A guy can really cook till his heart's content."

"Man oh fucking man, I have always had this fantasy of being done in a steam room," I stupidly said. "Just lying there on a long table like this one while guys work on me everywhere, especially these big size fourteen feet of mine."

Alex and Ronald looked at each other and a knowing glance seemed to pass between them.

"Size *fourteen?*" Alex asked me in disbelief. "You have size fucking fourteen feet?"

"Yeah man, triple fucking EEE, really gets me off to have my damned sexy big feet serviced, *with my stinking dress socks on no less, something about my feet being licked while wearing nylon socks gets me every damned time,"* I said and took another hearty gulp of my drink. "Not to mention other big parts of me, if you get my drift."

The two men seemed to consider what I had just said and then they looked at me lustfully.

"I'll tell you what Big guy Haynes," Alex began. "If you get yourself all stripped down to your dress socks and stretch your linebacker type body out on this table, right here, right now, we'll give you a good old fashioned steam bath. And when our buddies arrive for the grand opening party we'll send them down here to work you over a bit, *if you get my drift* I'll even tell them about your hot fetish for having your socked feet worked and serviced. If I may say so I find that to be truly fucking kinky. Hell, just thinking about it gives me a goddamned hard-on."

"How long would I have to stay in here?" I asked, looking longingly at the massage table. "As you said it gets really hot in here."

"As long as it takes to get you off, a few times," Alex said, taking my half empty glass from me. "And we'll make sure that you get plenty of water in between being steamed. We wouldn't want you getting dehydrated or passing out on us after all. But, you have to stay in here until you've gotten off a few times, *not just once or twice.*"

I placed my fingers under my chin and looked around the steam room.

"It sure is tempting," I said with a grin, my cock churning a bit in my suit pants. "I mean, I haven't gotten off in a few days and you're talking about getting me off *a few fucking times. GAWD,* okay, you guys got a deal. Where can I store my suit while I'm in here?"

"Right this way Sir," Ronald said, taking me by my upper arm and walking me out of the steam room. "Let's find you a locker."

Ronald brought me over to a bank of lockers a few feet from the steam room.

"You can chuck that fancy suit of yours in any one of these lockers," Ronald said, pointing to the lockers, my upper arm still held in his firm grip.

"Don't I need a combination lock or something?" I asked him, reaching up to begin undoing my tie.

"Nah, we're the only ones here tonight, not counting the guys coming to the party pretty soon," Ronald replied, finally letting go of my arm. "Your stuff will be safe enough in there."

"I can't believe I agreed to this," I said, slipping my tie off my shirt and hanging it in the open locker in front of us.

"It's going to be *the most intense* experience of your life Big guy Haynes," Ronald said lustfully as I shucked off my suit jacket followed quickly by my white shirt. "I mean, just think, you, laying all comfortable and stretched out in a steam room while guys service you everywhere, getting you off over and over. And I do hope that you're a man of your word and that you'll stay in there till you've gotten off more than a few times."

"I am a man of my word," I said, standing there now shirtless. "I agree to yours and Alex's conditions."

Ronald's jaw then dropped a few inches at the sight of my iron-like hugely muscular chest, over-sized pecs and washboard abs stomach area. I smiled as he breathlessly took in the sight of my hugely powerful biceps and triceps. But it was really my fat luscious looking man-sized tits that really captivated the fucking guy. He licked his lips over and over at the sight of them.

"Enjoying yourself Ronald?" I asked him with a sly looking grin as I stepped out of my slip-on wingtips, bent down to pick them up and placed them in the locker.

"Holy fuck man, how often do you workout?" Ronald asked me.

"As often as I can man, as often as I fucking can," I responded and unbuttoned my suit pants.

I stepped out of my suit pants, hung them up and shucked off my white briefs, revealing my horse cock. It hung semi hard, fat and extended between my tree-trunk like legs, my big juicy and sweaty balls hanging low behind it.

"*Fuck it man, you weren't joking when you mentioned big parts of you,*" Ronald said throatily, looking with awe at my pride and joy as I chucked my briefs into the locker and closed the door.

I stood before Ronald, now clad in just a pair of nylon, black calf length dress socks.

"Just remember what I told you man," I piped up, looking quickly down at my size fourteen socked feet and back at Ronald. "I like having my socked feet serviced. *That shit really, really gets me the fuck off.* And I always wear thin socks just like the stinkers I got on now. It makes it feel real fucking nice when a guy or a few work on my feet."

"No problem bud, no problem whatsoever," Ronald said, taking me again by my upper arm, this time purposely wedging his fingertips in one of my raunchy and smelly hairy armpits. "Let's get back to the steam room and start you cooking Big guy Haynes."

The way he said that last statement made me realize how I had literally handed myself over to him and Alex so that they could do with me as they saw it. It was like being in the control of men. We went back to the steam room and Alex, like Ronald took in the sight of me in awe, total awe.

"Fuck man, *you are built like a damned linebacker,*" Alex said breathlessly as Ronald walked me over to him. "And you sure as all hell do look real fucking sexy in just your socks Big guy Haynes."

I stood next to the massage table as the two men gave my nipples a squeeze and twist each.

"Oh yeah, that feels great you guys," I murmured.

"Fuck man, you've got the biggest and juiciest looking tits I've ever seen on a guy," Alex commented, practically breathlessly as he twisted one of my nipples like a bottle cap.

"You said it my man," I replied agreeably and gasped as the guys really tweaked the fucks out of my huge nips.

"And look at this," Alex said, reaching down and taking my big horse cock in his hand. "Fuck man, you are really blessed Big guy Haynes, you give new meaning to the expression hung like a bull."

I grinned and breathed heavily as the guy took my over-sized balls in his other hand, abandoning the nipple he had been toying with.

"Holy shit man, this pound of beef is throbbing like a thing alive in my hand," Alex said in awe, squeezing my huge cock and rolling my balls in his hand. "The fucking guys are just going to love making you shoot your load Big guy Haynes."

"Not as much as I'm going to love SHOOTING my load..." I said softly.

Then, Alex let go of my manhood and I stood docilely between my two buddies.

"You ready to start cooking?" Alex asked me, running the palm of his hand over the bottom of one of my man breasts, cupping it.

"Sure am Alex my man," I said with a grin. "You two can be the first ones to get me off."

"Let's help the man aboard," Alex said, gesturing at the tabletop.

Alex grabbed my arms as Ronald reached down to take my legs just above my calves. They hoisted me up off the floor and stretched me out nice and long on the table. Strong fuckers they had to be to be hoisting me let me tell you. With my arms resting at my sides and my legs slightly parted I looked up at my two buddies as they looked down at me, hungrily and with lust-filled eyes. My cock, semi hard pointed straight up and out and my tits pointed nice and meaty up at the ceiling. I looked like a damned linebacker relaxing during a grueling game. As I said earlier, what a sight I was.

"Comfortable?" Alex asked me as he and Ronald moved

stealthily to either side of the table.

"Yeah, feels real nice," I said with a smile. "Now why don't you two strip down, turn up the steam and start servicing me?"

"Sure thing Big guy Haynes," Alex said and tweaked one of my fat nipples, sending chills through me. "There's just *one more thing* to be taken care of."

"Oh yeah, what's that?" I asked.

"This," Alex said, reaching under the table at the same time Ronald did. "Now Ronald!!"

Before I could think to react or *do anything* they brought out from under the big table I was laying on two heavy-duty water-proof Velcro-like restraint straps. Both straps were connected to the table at the bottom of the structure. The two men quickly threw the center one over my upper body and worked fast at yanking it tight and getting me all helpless and trapped.

"H-hey!!" I gasped and lifted my head up off the table, watching as they secured the thick strap around my muscular upper body, pinning it down. *"WHAT* IS THIS? *What are you two fuckers up to here???"*
"Just making sure that you stick to your end of the bargain Big guy Haynes and making sure you stick to the table," Ronald chuckled, bringing out a smaller strap and fastening it quickly around one of my wrists, securing my hand down to the side of the table.

Fuck, I didn't even have a second to try to struggle my way out of their little trick trap. I have to admit however, that as they strapped me down good and fucking tight my horse cock pounded harder and harder.

"But I said I would stay in here till you guys said so," I complained bitterly, angry at myself for not having known better where Alex and Ronald were concerned. "There's no need for this shit, OH GAWD!!"

I knew from other guys, other buddies of mine who had fallen victim to Alex and Ronald. But I never thought that they would set their preying sights on me…and now I was their latest conquest.

"Believe me Big guy Haynes, it gets real fucking hot in here," Alex said, fastening the second strap over my stomach region and lower arms, pinning me there as well. "We don't want you getting any ideas of backing out of the deal once we start cooking you in here."

Fuckers, tricksters," I ranted angrily. "Some good buddies you two turned out to be.

Ronald stepped to the other side of the table and secured my other wrist with another short strap as Alex moved to the foot of the table.

"So tell me you big stud," Alex quipped, grabbing my socked ankles and leaning down real close to my smelly feet. "How do you want to be cooked, rare, medium well or *well fucking done?"*

Laughing, Alex slurped at my socked toes as Ronald secured short straps around my upper calves and then fastened a long heavy-duty Velcro-like strap over my muscular tree-trunk like legs. Damn, Alex slurping at my socked toes was sending chills through me already. Fuck it all, I was totally immobilized. Those two jokers had really gotten the drop on me...and I had fallen for it hook line and sinker.

"Perfect!" Alex said with satisfaction. "Our plan worked out real well."

"Your plan?" I barked at them. "You mean to say that you two clowns planned this shit?"

"Let's just say we hoped," Alex said, bent down and picked up my thick apple flavored health drink from under the table I was now on and strapped tightly down to.

The glass was still halfway full. Smiling, Alex took a small shaker from his pocket and sprinkled a goodly amount of the contents of the shaker into my glass.

"Still have to finish your drink Big guy Haynes," Alex said a fiendish looking grin on his face.

"What is that that you sprinkled in there man?" I asked him angrily. "I'm not drinking that if it's drugs you put in there."

"Not to worry you big stallion," Alex said. "We wouldn't do anything to hurt you. We're going to do plenty to frustrate you, but definitely not hurt you. And this drink isn't going in the front end either."

Ronald grabbed a lever that was under the end of the table and suddenly said table was hoisted halfway up, my head now hanging upside down, my legs in the air.

"OHHHHH JEEZ, wh-what is this?" I garbled miserably. "What the fuck are you two up to?"

"The powder I sprinkled in your drink is a mixture of potent herbs from the Orient, multi-vitamins and professional gainer's powdered milk," Alex said, holding up my glass as the powder settled in my apple drink. "All adding up to one of the most powerful aphrodisiacs on the face of God's earth."

From what I guessed to be a storage area under the table Ronald brought out a funnel, a funnel with an unusually long hollow stem.

"And we're going to feed it to you now Big guy," Alex said, looking menacingly between my legs at my exposed and slightly open raunchy and stinking asshole.

"OH no, *no,*" I pleaded desperately.

"You are going to be hornier than ever before in your life Big guy Haynes," Ronald said, moving the stem of the funnel toward my hole.

"EEEERRRRHHHH GOD," I seethed as Ronald slid the long hollow stem of the funnel slowly into my gaping asshole. "OHHHHHH you fuckers!! The least you guys could have done was lubricated me a bit down there."

"And miss out on the fun of watching you squirm so sexily on that table?" Alex asked me meanly. "No fucking way no how you gorgeous stud."

When the funnel was good and wedged inside me Alex stepped next to his prank playing buddy and held the glass over it.

"You ready for this Big guy Haynes?" Alex asked me.

"I-I suppose I don't have much choice in the matter now, do I?" I replied miserably.

Chuckling, Alex said "no" and slowly poured the now aphrodisiac spiked drink through the funnel and into my rectal hole.

"OOOHHHHHHH fuuuucccccckkkk, wh-what a sensation!" I garbled as I felt the thick creamy liquid flooding my hole and seeping into me.

"Down the hatch and right into your bloodstream Big guy Haynes," Alex said with a grin.

As Alex poured the drink into me Ronald slowly thrust the long stem of the funnel in my hole, fucking me with the damned thing. My cock grew harder and harder, stiffer and stiffer between my legs, pulsing and twitching with a life all its own. The sounds and feelings of squishing filled the air as my hole became sopped up with the apple drink.

"AAAYYYRRRR JEEZ," I panted. "I-I'm feeling real strange now you guys."

"That's the aphrodisiac taking effect," Alex explained as he poured the drink some more through the funnel. "You'll be feeling it in your cock any second now..."

Sure enough, the fucking prankster was right. As my hole literally sucked up the drink it was being fed my cock pounded harder and harder, in need of *real* release.

"OOOHHH FUCK, OH GOD, I hope one of you tricksters is planning on getting me off real soon," I panted. "Man oh man, I'm sweating already and the steam isn't even on yet."

"Well you see Big guy Haynes, that's another reason we had to get you strapped down the way you are," Ronald said, thrusting the funnel in and out of my hole, teasing me and fucking me madly with the device, driving me crazy.

"What the fuck are you talking about man?" I asked, a feeling of dread starting to fill me.

"We're not going to get you off for a while, a long while bud," Alex explained as he poured the last of my drink into me. "We want you to be real worked up and in a real frothy lather when we do finally get you off, *after* our "Grand Opening" party is over. Let's see how long we can keep you balanced on the sexual edge."

That said Alex held up my empty glass and Ronald slowly pulled the funnel stem from my sopped hole.

"OOOOHHHH fuck, fuck," I grunted as the funnel came out of my hole, all slimy and slippery.

I farted once and the residue of my drink splattered onto the table. Laughing and cackling meanly Alex and Ronald slid their fingers in and out of my gaping hole, prodding it and digging around meanly in there.

"OHHHHH GAWD, y-you fuckers tricked me big time," I gasped angrily. "Pl-please you guys, I-I need to shoot my damned load!"

"We know you do," Alex said, stepping to the foot of the table. "And that's why you will be so glad when we do finally get you off, *a few hours from now.*"

Ronald slid his fingers out of my hole as Alex pulled on the lever under the table, returning the table to its normal position. I lay there stretched out, helpless, horny as all hell and feeling real fucking stupid. I knew of Alex and Ronald's antics and I knew that I should have known better than to fall for one of their sadistic jokes.

"B-but you said that your party buddies would be coming down here and getting me off more than a few times," I said in an insisting manner. (Anything at this point to get someone, anyone to jack me the fuck off.)

"We sort of bent the truth on that too you gorgeous stud," Alex said, hooking his hands tightly around my socked ankles. "They'll be coming down here to work you over, if you get my drift. We'll allow them to work your feet, your tits, your balls, anywhere they want to go, *except your cock!"*

I clenched my teeth in anger as Alex leaned down and ran his tongue over the tips of my socked toes on my right foot.

"Fucking bastards, you really *tricked* me!!" I seethed. "Let me up off this table, now!!"

"You want another good dose of the aphrodisiac up your ass Big guy Haynes?" Ronald taunted me, holding up my empty glass.

"N-no, I-I'm so fucking horny that it's making me crazy!!" I replied desperately.

"Then take it like a man when we do get you off you'll be thankful for the entire experience," Alex said and ecstatically suckled my socked toes, sending chills through me. "Believe me, after we kept that sailor boy tied up in that bathroom stall at our bar he was so milked by night's end that he actually came back for more…as will you Big guy Haynes."

"Oh yeah, just eat my feet you bastard, it's the least you can do after tricking me the way you did," I gasped angrily.

As Alex worked my feet Ronald leaned down and slurped one of my fat tits into his mouth…

"Hooooooo fuck, hell of a way to treat a guy you call your good buddy," I said angrily. "Get him all horny, hot and bothered and then "not" get him off…"

Ronald stopped working my meaty tit and wrapped a hand around my huge pulsing nine inches of cock.

"Oh yeah, fuck yeah, changed your mind eh you miserable bastard?" I asked him hopefully. "Start stroking my meat crank man, *please!!"*

"The only thing this meat crank is going to be spurting for a good while tonight is piss Big guy Haynes, to be exact," Ronald said meanly, squeezing my cock, but not stroking the guy. "From the way you'll be cooking in here you will need lots of water and believe me you'll be pissing your guts out."

Ronald let go of my cock and slurped one of my big tits back into his mouth as Alex went on and on licking and slurping at my stinking socked feet. After a while the two men stopped working my feet and tits and they walked to the door of the steam room. My cock was now fully hard and pointing straight up at the ceiling, twitching and oozing what would be the first of many droplets of pre cum.

"Okay Big guy Haynes," Alex said, looking at his watch. "Our buddies should be here within the next ten or fifteen minutes or so. That should be more than enough time to start you cooking in here."

Ronald, standing next to Alex at the door placed his hand on the valve that controlled the steam. He turned the valve slowly to the section marked "High Intense Heat."

"OH GOD, you fuckers," I whispered, realizing too late that I had gotten in way over my head.

The two men exited the steam room, the door closing silently behind them. The steam started filling the room and caressing me, nice and hot and getting me good and sweaty...

Within a few minutes I was thoroughly soaked in sweat from head to socked toes. Thick beads of moisture slid off my forehead and into my dreadlocked styled hair, my thick chest hair was matted to my hugely muscular chest making my tits look even bigger than they were and my curly pubic hairs were sopped in sweat as well. I breathed as evenly as possible, fearing that I would pass out from the intense heat. My socks were sweat-soaked, stinking and stuck to my feet. It would be a pleasure when some guys got in there to service them for me that was for sure. For whatever the fuck the reason I've always thoroughly enjoyed the feeling of a guy's tongue as it slid over my nylon socked feet. And on that night I would get plenty of just that, plus a whole lot more...

After ten minutes of being steamed I was in a state of dizzy ecstasy mixed with limbo, in other words my damned head was spinning. Sweat covered my muscular black body from head to socked toes at that point. I needed water like never before in my life and I was beginning to wonder *when* someone, anyone would come through the door to the steam room. My horse cock pounded big and beefy between my muscular thighs, pointing straight up at the ceiling. Glistening thick droplets of pre cum were oozing and oozing from it. I was awash with goose bumps and chills as Alex's aphrodisiac slid through my bloodstream. Man, I was miserable, horny and in a lather already. And fuck it all, I still had hours of this shit ahead of me. As the steam caressed me and poured liberally over me I smiled thinly...

The first two of Alex and Ronald's friends to come to the steam room and work me over for a while were two of their good buddies named Dennis and Howard. I knew the two of them from past parties with Alex and Ronald and to put it bluntly they were as much the jokers as Alex and Ronald are. Both of them pretty well built, Dennis with short blond hair and Howard with dark brown hair they both entered the steam room wearing nothing but towels around their waists.

"Whoo, it really is fucking hot in here!" Dennis crowed as they entered the steam room. "Alex and Ronald weren't kidding!"

"And look what else they weren't kidding about," Howard said merrily as they sidled up next to the table, moving quickly to my socked feet. "Our good buddy, Big guy Haynes, all strapped down for our feasting pleasure. Never thought I would see the day when *he* would be in a position like this."

"That goes double for me Howard," I said shrilly.

Smiling through the clouds upon clouds of thick steam the two men each wrapped their hands around one of my big smelly feet.

"Feeling good Big guy Haynes?" Dennis asked me, squeezing and caressing my right foot at the arch, pressing his thumbs against the meaty bottom of it.

"Y-yeah, jus-just what I've always wanted," I whispered breathlessly. "F-fuckers, get busy working my feet."

"I have to admit Big guy Haynes, I've always had a fantasy about servicing these big size fourteen stinking feet of yours," Howard mused, leaning down and sliding the tip of his tongue across my socked toes. "I just never imagined I would get my wish fulfilled in a steam room, with you all strapped down and in just your socks no less."

"And lets not forget that strapped rhymes with *trapped,*" Dennis said meanly. "Big guy Haynes can't stop us from doing *just what the fuck we want to him, for as long as we want.*"

I lifted my head and watched through blurred vision as my two so called buddies slathered their dripping tongues over my socked toes, sucked my socked toes and slurped and licked at the sides and bottoms of my big feet. They pulled some of the cloth of my socks away from my toes and with their eyes shut in ecstasy and their hands wrapped tightly around my feet they sucked heartily at my smelly socks.

"OH YEAH, that feels real nice, treat my feet and socks with respect you bastards," I whispered huskily as I lay there sweating like mad. "It's the least you guys can do for me."

My cock pounded big and hard between my legs and more and more pre cum oozed from my wide sexy slit. (What would be done to my wide sexy slit doesn't bear talking about, but you'll know soon enough.) Dennis and Howard moved their tongues over the tops of my feet, slowly, so slowly, their hands wrapped around my upper calves as they did so…

"*Gawd, just look at the size of the meat between his legs,*" Howard said in awe. "I wish we could steal a few sucks off it, but Alex and Ronald said he's not to be allowed to cum."

"Hmm, maybe we're not allowed to suck him and get him off," Dennis mused. "But we sure can frustrate the fuck out of him a little more by just holding that enormous rod in our mouths for a few seconds each."

"Oh no, no, that would be worse than doing nothing at all to my damned meat," I garbled miserably as the two men flicked their tongues over and over my socks, working their way up my calves.

Just watching the two guys tongue worship my feet was enough to make me feel as I could shoot my load without even having my cock touched. But alas, that was not to be the case. I'm not one of those guys who can shoot his load just by thinking about it.

"Kiss 'em you bastards, kiss my damned feet," I seethed in the heat as sweat poured off me in what seemed like rivers.

Dennis and Howard planted small delicate kisses on the sides and tops of my feet, holding them tightly by my calves.

"Fuck, tell me Howard, how fucking often did you think about getting at those stinking feet of mine?" I asked breathlessly.

"Just about every time we all went out after work, at every party I ever say you at," Howard said in between slurping and kissing my feet. "And you, you fucker, you always teased me without even realizing it man. You always crossed your leg or rested your foot on your knee, showing just a little bit of that sexy black skin of yours just above your damned sock."

Looking at me hungrily Howard snapped the elastic in my socks against my skin.

"Well, looks like teasing time is over for now eh Big guy Haynes?" Howard asked me, squeezing the upper part of my left foot as Dennis sucked the toes on my right foot as if they were a cock.

"OHHHHHHHH GOD," I whispered breathlessly.

"But I sure do love your big feet Big guy Haynes," Howard said and kissed the tips of my toes.

A short while later, after really slurping and sucking the fuck out of my stinking socked feet Dennis and Howard sidled up to the center of the table. My huge cock pointed straight up at the ceiling, pre cum oozing from my slit like crazy and sweat glistening all over the shaft as it throbbed.

"Fuck man, this guy has a cock likened to the size of ponies," Dennis said hungrily.

"Remember, we can't make him cum," Howard said, as Dennis leaned down closer to my pride and joy, sniffing my cock a bit as he did so.

"Relax Howard, he isn't going to cum, but I am going to give him some payback for the way he used to cock tease us with those big feet of his."

That said Dennis slurped the crown and just the first few inches of my massive man-meat into his mouth. He pressed his tongue against the side of it and simply held it tight in his craw, not sucking me.

"OOOHHHHHHHHH, JEEZ, but th-this is a shitty ass thing to do to a guy you call your good buddy," I rasped, my head arched back. "I-I never cock teased you guys on purpose Dennis, OHHHHHHH fuckkkkk!!!"

My cock half in Dennis' mouth drove me batty made my head spin and even caused me to salivate like crazy. GAWD, what a sight that was. I wasn't even able to pulsate my pelvis to get my cock moving in the guy's mouth, a last hope to try to make myself shoot that damned load. Worse was when Dennis let my pole slip out of his mouth and Howard bent down to take it into his mouth. Fuck, fuck, fuck, why did Alex and Ronald have to feed me that damned aphrodisiac?

"Easy man, don't suck him," Dennis said, moving back down to my feet to give them a few final sucks, slurps and kisses.

As Dennis again tongue worshipped my feet and Howard held my cock in his craw I nearly flew off that table. Thank the gods I was strapped down good and fucking tight huh? *Not!!!* I curled my trapped hands into meaty fists and whispered that I was extremely thirsty and that I had to piss. Howard let my cock slip out of his mouth as Dennis dashed to get a quart-sized bottle of cool mineral water. In less than a minute I was gratefully sipping down the cool water. Dennis held the bottle to my lips as Howard held my head up by the back of my neck, his hand caressing me and toying with my sweat soaked dreadlocks at the same time.

"There you go Big guy Haynes, drink it down bud," Dennis said soothingly. "Alex and Ronald said we were to give you as much water as you wanted."

As I sipped down the water Howard kissed me gently on the cheek.

"Fucking gorgeous stud you are Big guy Haynes," Howard whispered. "When this is all over you're more than welcome to come and spend some time at our place. We'll make you shoot your load all night."

I smiled thinly in between slaking my thirst as Howard again kissed me on the cheek...

When I was no longer thirsty I realized that I had drunk the entire quart-sized bottle of mineral water.

"G-GOOD GOD, *God almighty, but I have to piss like a racehorse!*" I seethed in a high pitched tone of voice.

Smiling, the two men again moved to the center of the table, Dennis with the empty bottle in his hand.

"Alex and Ronald also said that we were to allow you to piss as much as you wanted as well," Dennis said and placed the tip of the bottle over my wide sexy slit.

He gently moved my cock to a prone straight position and then said, "Piss." As I pissed and pissed like crazy into the bottle Howard pushed the towel around his waist aside and took his crusty hardness in hand.

"Man oh fucking man Dennis, working this guy over in this steam room has made me hornier than a bitch in heat," Howard said and began stroking himself.

He was hornier than a bitch in heat? The fucker should have known half of how I was feeling at that moment. I mean, give a guy an aphrodisiac, and through his anal canal no less, get him all worked up and hold his hard cock in your mouth and NOT let him cum??? Fuck, *let's talk about horny...*"

"AHHHHHH!!!" I breathed and sighed heavily, relief filling me as I pissed and pissed into the water bottle.

"Shit, it seems like this guy has a geysers worth of piss in him," Dennis mused as Howard stood there stroking his hard cock, watching in awe as I pissed and pissed.

Suddenly, Howard hoisted himself up onto the table over me, straddling my huge chest, his hard white boy cock staring me in the face.

"Fuck man, suck my cock you gorgeous stud," Howard commanded, sweating like crazy as he slid his hardness into my mouth.

"Mmmmmmmffff…" I sputtered around his cock as my big lips began working their magic on it.

"OHHHHHH yeah, feels fucking great," Howard ranted as my mouth made love to his cock, he leaned forward, plowing my mouth still more with his erection and grabbing my dreadlocks in his fingers and thumbs. "OHHHHH fuck, maybe you're not allowed to shoot your load Big guy Haynes, but we sure as fuck can shoot ours. Still thirsty you gorgeous fuck? Well, I'll give you something to drink any second now."

I looked up at the guy through the haze of steam as he fucked my mouth royally. He held onto my sweat sopped dreadlocks, gently pulling my head back and forth for better rhythm on his cock. As I sucked and sucked Howard's somewhat big meat I finished pissing (for the moment) and Dennis put the water bottle down on the floor against the wall. It would be one of many water bottles containing my piss that night. Dennis, watching as Howard made me eat his cock pushed his towel aside and grabbed his cock in hand, aiming it at my stinking socked feet.

"Yeah, that's it Howard, fuck his throat, fill his gullet with your mess," Dennis said breathlessly.

"Yeah, I'm getting there now Dennis, fuck but I'm getting there," Howard seethed passionately and slid his cock further into my craw. "OHHHHHHH yeah, fucking A!! Never shot my load in a steam room before!"

And what a load it was. Working my feet and teasing my cock had made Howard shoot a load big enough to choke a horse.

"RRRRRMMFFFF!!!" I gasped as I quickly scoffed down rope after rope of the guy's thick creaminess.

"OH yeah, feels fucking great you stud," Howard barked in my face, letting go of my dreadlocks.

As Howard's cock slid out of my mouth and I lowered my head back down onto the table Dennis shot his load; all over my damned socked feet. What a sight that was let me tell you, something so hot about thick white creamy sperm all over my black socks…

"OHHHHHH yeah, my turn Howard, my fucking turn!!" Dennis crooned in the heat of the steam room.

He splattered his white boy mess all over my socked feet, over my toes and it slid down the fronts and backs of my feet. I wiggled my toes and it made the sexy mess all over my feet look even more comical somehow.

"GAWD, but you fuckers have made me really fucking jealous," I garbled as Howard climbed down off the table, the taste of his cock and cum still fresh in my mouth.

"We'll leave my splooge on his feet for the next guys who come in here to lick off," Dennis suggested to Howard as they adjusted their towels back around their waists.

"Sounds like a good idea to me," Howard said agreeably. "Come on, let's get out of here. The heat is becoming too much for me now."

"Yeah, we can always come back later for seconds," Dennis laughed meanly. "The way Alex and Ronald plan it, Big guy Haynes will still be here."

Laughing, the two men exited the steam room and headed to the showers...

"OHHHHHH fuck," I whispered miserably as my cock twitched long and hard between my legs, pointing straight up at the ceiling. *"Jeez, I have to piss again..."*

The next two guys who came into the steam room were spanking Master Jeff and his slave boy Chris. When I saw them enter the steam room a feeling of dread came over me. Master Jeff, a five foot eight inch tall guy with brown hair, brown eyes and a slightly muscular build had always made jokes and mean cracks about having me in a position akin to the one I was now in. Master Jeff is a true S&M dominant. Spanking guys and disciplining them is his passion and the way I've heard it told he keeps his slave boy's ass cheeks good and red, just to keep the guy in line and to always remind him of whom is the master in their relationship. Master Jeff's slave boy Chris is a sinister looking guy of about five feet nine inches with short cropped brown hair and brown eyes. He has a lanky but well toned build from all the cardio-vascular exercises he does. Fucking guy always had a mean looking glint in his eyes when he saw me at social gatherings or parties that we all happened to be at.

Like Dennis and Howard before them they entered the steam room wearing nothing but towels around their waists.

"Oh on, *oh fuck,"* I whispered, knowing that I was really in for some nastiness where these two were concerned.

"Well, well, well, Big fucking guy Haynes," Slave boy Chris said, sidling up to the table, a bloody Mary in his hand, a stalk of celery and a stirrer in the glass. "Now this is what I call a party, a real fucking party. When Alex told me that he and Ronald had you strapped down to a table down here in the steam room I thought for sure that he was yanking my chain. But, *but,* here you are, all trussed up, helpless, totally fucking helpless and unable to stop us from doing whatever the fuck we want to you."

"H-hey guys," I said softly. "How's the party going up there?"

"It's going, but you're obviously not," Master Jeff said to me in reply, taking my big sweaty bull sized balls in his hand as Slave boy Chris walked down to the end of the table, to my feet to be exact. "Tell me, how did a big fucking stud like you get himself into a situation like this?"

"F-fucking Alex and Ronald pulled a-a fast one on me Master Jeff," I replied breathlessly as he fondled and toyed with my massive sized balls.

"Lucky for us I suppose," Master Jeff said as Slave boy Chris leaned down over my cum splattered feet.

"Hey, who the fuck shot their load all over your big sexy feet Big guy Haynes?" Slave boy Chris asked me, trailing a finger over my toes.

"D-Dennis," I responded, lifting my head up off the table and looking down at Slave boy Chris as he began sucking Dennis' cum off my socked toes.

Master Jeff let go of my testicles and pressed a hand against my forehead, pushing my head back down onto the table.

"You just lay back and let my boy work on those big stinking feet of yours Big guy," Master Jeff said, instantly taking charge and looking me over. "I sure wish those guys had strapped you down on your stomach though. That way I would be able to give that sexy black butt of yours a good old fashioned spanking."

It was at that moment that I noticed that Master Jeff had a round leather paddle stuck in the towel around his waist. Slave boy Chris had put his drink down on the table between my spread feet and was busy now sucking and licking my socked feet with real gusto.

"But, I do suppose other parts of you will do just as well for a good spanking," Master Jeff said, giving one of my rock hard pecs and nipples a hard squeeze, sending chills through me, adding to the chills that Slave boy Chris' tongue was sending through my socked feet.

"Oh fuck man, y-you're not planning on spanking me in here are you Master Jeff?" I garbled miserably. "Th-that would really be a shitty thing to do to me. And not to mention that I have to piss like crazy."

"My slave boy will take care of that for you shortly in a way that you will not believe," Master Jeff said snidely, taking his leather paddle in hand. "But for getting yourself into such a humiliating position I think some punishment is called for Big guy Haynes. I'll work fast you gorgeous fuck, seeing as I really can't deal with this heat."

With a mean looking smile on his face Master Jeff raised his paddle...

"OHHHHHHH FUCK!!!" I grunted angrily as he brought the paddle down good and hard on my left pec. "OWWWWWWWW!!! I d-didn't come here to have the fuck spanked out of me man!!"

In reply Master Jeff gave my left pec another two hard swats with his paddle. With my head raised off the table I watched as glistening sweat flew off me each time the fucker spanked me.

"AAARRHHHHH!!!" I ranted as the swats to the same spot over and over began to sting like the devil.

With each swat Master Jeff increased the intensity of the blows. When my left pec had suffered a good twenty mean swats Master Jeff began meanly paddling my right one. The sounds of the paddle connecting with flesh filled the steam room. As Master Jeff worked me over with the paddle his slave boy Chris was busy sucking, slurping and feasting like crazy on my stinking socked toes. The sensation of my toes being sucked combined with the spanking I was getting was intoxicating yet excruciatingly painful all at the same time.

"AWWWWWWWWW!!! FUCKER!!!" I seethed and arched my head back on the table as Master Jeff swatted and swatted my right pec, intensifying the blows each time. "OHHHHHHH SHHHHHIIITTT!!! And all I came here for tonight was to check the goddamned gym out that Alex and Ronald had opened."

"Well, from what we heard you checked it out, checked in and aren't leaving any time soon Stud," Slave boy Chris cackled from the foot end of the table, his hands wrapped tightly around my big feet.

"Vulture!!" I ranted at Slave boy Chris as he slid his lips over the side of my feet. "OWWWWWWWW!!!!"

"Just wait till I mash those big fat tits of yours a few times and my slave boy here sucks 'em back up for you," Master Jeff chided me meanly and began alternating back and forth swatting and spanking my poor tingling pecs. "Each time he sucks 'em up I'm going to mash them down again."

Before I could utter a word pf protest Master Jeff brought his paddle down hard on one of my big tits while at the same time his vulture of a slave boy decided to slather his tongue over my big sweaty and stinking balls. Jeez, he didn't even ask his master for permission…

"OOOOOOHHHHH sssshiiiittt, ea-easy with my tits you fucker!!" I screamed in a man's pain, the sweat pouring off me in rivers at that point, my entire body bathed in it.

It was horrible to watch (and feel) as Master Jeff really put the screws to my poor nipples, whapping them good and fucking hard over and over, mashing them as he said he was going to do. His slave boy seemed to be in a state of pure ecstasy as he licked, slurped and kissed my big balls over and over and over. My cock throbbed wildly between my legs, more than aching for release at that point. Fuck, I wondered just how long it would be before Master Jeff stopped torturing my tits and ordered his slave boy to suck 'em back up again.

"MMM, big black balls, hung like a fucking horse this guy is," Slave boy Chris crooned, bent over at my crotch as he tongue bathed my balls, slurping the sweat off them again and again.

"AAAYYYRRR!!" I cried out loudly as Master Jeff alternately whapped and paddled my poor tits.

Fuck, shitty thing to paddle a guy's tits let me tell you.

"Okay Boy, get off those balls of his and get over here," Master Jeff said commandingly to his slave. "I need these tits of his sucked up and really sore for the next round of spanking they're in for."

"Yes Master Jeff," Slave boy Chris said and quickly did his master's bidding.

With my head raised off the table I watched and swooned in ecstasy as the guy sucked and slurped alternately at my big fat mashed tits. Fuck man, that slave boy sucked my tits like they were a pair of cocks on my big muscular chest, running his hands up and down my strapped down torso at the same time. Master Jeff looked at me adoringly as his slave boy did his work on my tits.

"Fuck it all man, my good buddies," I said with a grin. "You guys love having me in this fucked up position. Man oh man, I am a feast fit for a king like this."

About five minutes later Master Jeff ordered his slave boy off my tits and back to my feet as he raised his paddle high. My tits were sucked up to two erasers-like nubs on my big chest, two perfect targets for Master Jeff's damned paddle.

"AAAYYYRRRR!!!" I screamed in pain anew as he again went to work paddling and mashing my poor tits, sweat flying off my chest with each blow. "PL-please man, th-this is too much now!!" So, as the heat bathed and tortured me, as Slave boy Chris slurped and sucked at my socked feet and as Master Jeff paddled the fuck out of my poor tits my cock throbbed and throbbed like crazy...

It was a good ten to fifteen minutes later when Master Jeff stopped paddling my poor tits and pecs. By the time he stopped I was a screaming crazy mess. There were welts on my pecs and my tits had been mashed down again, only to be sucked back up and made really sore by that vulture slave boy of his. I lay there gasping and panting for breath as the two men stood by the massage table sipping bottles of cool mineral water. They teased and tormented me by spilling some of their cool water over my body. That really shocked the fuck out of me and got me to gasp even louder.

"Fuckers, paddle a guy's tits and pecs," I seethed miserably. "That's a lousy thing to do."

"Just wait till we're cooled down some and I paddle your muscle boy thighs," Master Jeff said meanly and took a long swig of mineral water.

"And just wait till I make you eat my cock," Slave boy Chris added and moved to the center of the table, namely right over my huge throbbing cock and bulging balls.

"Now, did I hear Big guy Haynes say he had to piss earlier?" Chris asked, holding up the thin stirrer straw from his drink.

"He sure as hell said that," Master Jeff said.

"OHHHH fuck, no, no, *not this you bastard!!*" I roared maniacally.

Master Jeff and I watched; he in awe and me in pain as Slave boy Chris slowly inserted his stirrer into my cock slit.

"OOOHHHHHHHH fuck, y-you guys are going to make me insane before the night is over!!" I screeched wildly.

"When I start sucking you start pissing you big stud," Slave boy Chris said, twisting and turning the stirrer into my slit, fucking my piss hole with it.

"Fuck, fuck, *fuck, hell of a way to make a guy piss,*" I whimpered miserably, tears of agony threatening to spill from my eyes.

Then Slave boy Chris wrapped his lips around the stirrer and I did as I had been told, I started pissing.

"AAAAYYYY GAWD, what a fucked up sensation," I cried as my piss trickled through the thin straw and Slave boy Chris scoffed it down greedily.

"D-did you put him up to this Master Jeff?" I asked, looking up at Master Jeff through the haze of steam.

"No, that slave boy of mine has got a hell of an imagination," Master Jeff replied and then my tears did flow.

There was no holding them back. I cried for my stupidity in being duped into this mess. I cried from the feeling of utter helplessness that had enveloped me. I cried because of the mental and physical tortures I was being forced to endure and most of all, most of fucking all I cried because I wanted to shoot my load, just one that was all I asked.

"AAAYYYYRRR!!!" I shrieked, as Slave boy Chris siphoned my piss slowly through the stirrer.

When I was done pissing Chris left the stirrer wedged in my cock hole, just to drive me even crazier I suppose. Master Jeff then got busy spanking my thighs as Chris again went to work servicing my big smelly socked feet…

The night was young bud. My miseries had just begun…

Massive amounts of sweat flew off my thighs as Master Jeff spanked the hell out of them with his leather paddle.

"AAARRRHHHHH!!!" I roared mightily.

"Like I said Big guy Haynes, I sure wish they had strapped you down on your stomach," Master Jeff teased me and whapped the living fuck out of my thighs alternately. "Spanking your inner thighs would hurt and sting a hundred times more, take my word for it. And I would have loved to be able to have gotten at spanking that sexy ass of yours as well…"

"I-I-I'IIOWWWWWWWW!! I'll just have to take your word for it about my inner thighs Master Jeff!" I gasped miserably.

A while later Master Jeff had stopped beating my thighs. Like the other parts of me that he had pummeled they were stinging and tingling like crazy. Slave boy Chris stopped servicing my big feet wrapped his hands around them and looked at me across the table I was strapped down on.

"Fuck man, I could lick and slurp at these stinking feet of his all night long Master Jeff Sir," Chris said. "But the heat is really starting to get to me in here."

With a mean looking grin on his face Chris moved away from my feet and like Howard did earlier he climbed up on the table, straddling my big muscular chest. He pushed his towel aside and dangled his hard white boy cock in my face.

"Come on you gorgeous fuck, suck my meat," Chris said meanly and shoved his hardness in my mouth.

With no choice whatsoever in the matter I sucked cock like my life depended on it. Slave boy Chris' cock was pretty thick and long at the same time, a lot bigger than Howard's was that was for sure. Not bad for a white boy cock I thought humorously.

"OHHHHH yeah, yeah, fucking great cock sucker you are Big guy Haynes," Slave boy Chris panted.

As I sucked Slave boy Chris' cock Master Jeff (mercifully) took the stirrer out of my damned piss hole.

"Mmmmmmmm," I crooned and sucked harder on Chris' cock as the stirrer was slowly pulled from my slit.

I felt the need to piss begin to start again.

"OOOOHHHH fuck, I'm getting close already you stud," Chris panted louder, thrusting his cock deeper and deeper in my craw. "OHHHHH fucking A, yeah man!!"

Slave boy Chris spewed a good hefty load of white boy juices and forced me to chow down on and swallow just about every drop of it. I imagined he had oodles of the stuff stored up in his balls. I guessed that Master Jeff did not allow his slave to cum all that often, so when he finally did it was plentiful.

"Yeah, that's it Stud, drink my love juice," Chris barked at me. "Fuck man, I drank your rancid piss after all."

When he was done his cock slipped slowly from between my lips and he hopped down off the table.

"I'm about ready to get out of here Master Jeff Sir," Slave boy Chris said, adjusting his towel back around his waist. "The heat is too much at this point. Unless you want to stay to spank him some more that is…"

"No, but I do want to stay long enough to force him to guzzle another quart of mineral water," Master Jeff said, holding up a fresh bottle. "This poor fuck is going to be pissing his guts out."

As Master Jeff held the tip of the bottle to my lips Slave boy Chris held my head up by the back of my neck, his hands in my sweat-sopped dreadlocks. I sipped down the water and with each swallow my cock pounded piss hard like crazy.

"Drink up Big guy Haynes", Chris said and kissed me on the forehead. "*You need* that water, seeing as you're going to be in here for quite some more time tonight."

When I was done drinking the water Master Jeff put the empty bottle down on the floor. He and Slave boy Chris wished me a fun evening and told me that they had to go and shower, get dressed and get back to the party upstairs in the gym. With a look of dismay on my face I watched the two men exit the steam room. It was about ten to fifteen minutes later when those two so-called buddies of mine, Alex and Ronald came into the steam room. By then I had been in there for more than two hours or so. The steam was so thick that one could barely see one's hand in front of his face. I was matted and drenched in sweat and the cushion on the massage table I lay on was sopped in it also.

"Whoooo, it sure is hot in here," Alex said as he and Ronald entered the steam room. "And what a party, fuck man, and best grand opening party I've ever seen, even better than when we opened "The Local" bar."

Alex stepped over to the steam control valve and turned it to the "Off" position.

"Fuckers, it's about time you jokers got down here to let me out of here," I snarled at them as the steam slowly cleared. "Fuck it all you guys, I am beyond cooked."

They stepped over to the table and stood on either side of it, Alex with a tall glass of the apple flavored health drink in his hand.

"Yeah, you sure are well done Big guy Haynes," Ronald laughed, trailing a fingertip down my muscular chest, over my nipples and poking it into my belly button, sending chills and thrills through my being, slightly tickling me as well. "And just look at that fucking man gland of yours, totally stiff, totally fucking rigid."

"But let you out of here Trevor?" Alex asked me, shaking his head "no" from side to side. "You have a way to go and besides, the party upstairs is just getting going."

"B-but, but," I stammered. "But you've had your fun with me man. Shit, I've been sucked at, made to piss, I'm hornier than ever before in my life and that bastard Master Jeff paddled the fuck out of me. His fucking slave boy, that vulture Chris drank my piss through a stirrer. Fucking guy man, that really hurt let me tell you."

Alex and Ronald looked across the table at each other and

grinned meanly.

"Come on you fuckers," I pleaded. "If, if you're not going to let me out of here then at least have the decency to get me off. Look at my big horse cock, fuck man; I'm harder than hard, harder tan steel here. Not to mention the fact that I have to piss like crazy again."

"You don't get to shoot a load or a few till the party upstairs is over Trevor," Alex said to me, giving one of my fat nipples a squeeze, sending more blinding chills through me. "We just came down here to check on you, make sure you're okay and to give you a break and a drink."

Smiling, Alex held up the glass filled with the apple flavored health drink.

"Well, Master Jeff just fed me a bottle of mineral water so I'm really not all that thirsty guys," I said.

"But Big guy, it's the same drink that we gave you earlier," Ronald said, moving to the end of the table and grasping the lever underneath it.

"Oh no, *no, you bastards,*" I grunted miserably and throatily as Ronald hoisted the table up to a diagonal position, getting my legs in the air and my asshole visible. "Th-that would be too much at this point. Not another dose of that damned aphrodisiac!"

"You know it's no wonder you're a topnotch executive boy where you work Trevor," Alex said, taking the long stemmed funnel from the storage area under the table. "You are just too fucking smart for your own good."

"OHHHHHHHHH shiiiiiiiittttt!!!" I snarled, as Ronald slid the stem of the funnel into my hole and Alex stood ready to pour the potent aphrodisiac-laced drink into me.

"Man, after this drink he's going to be drunk as a skunk on the stuff," Alex laughed as the stuff trickled into my damned stinking hole. "He's going to be making promises he won't be able to keep in exchange for letting him shoot his load."

Fuck, fuck; fuck it all, my damned hole betrayed me by sucking and suckling the stuff greedily into me and down into my innards. I lifted my head up as chills of sheer and blinding ecstasy coursed through me. My cock was oozing massive droplets of pre cum and piss into my thick pubic bush and over my stomach area. My huge black sweaty balls were tingling like crazy in my sac, no doubt filled to bursting capacity with my juices at that point…

"OHHHHH you blasted fuckers," I garbled. "Fucking jokesters!"

When they were done feeding me the drink; and they had poured every drop of it into me I should add Ronald slowly pulled the funnel from my hole. I didn't fart this time. Alex returned the table to its rightful position and put the empty glass down on the floor.

"Feeling good stud?" Alex asked me, again squeezing one of my nipples real hard, giving it a twist this time.

"I-I-I feel crazy man," I gasped. "Shit, *but I really need to shoot my load now!!*"

The two men laughed merrily, leaned down and they each slurped one of my big nipples into their mouths...

"OHHHHHH yeah, real-really fucking glad you two are sucking the fuck out of my big man sized tits guys," I panted and heaved under the tight straps. "But I sure as all fucks do wish that one of you would give my horse cock a few strokes. He sure could use it right about now."

Never before in all my life had I been this horny. Never had I felt so fucking balanced on the edge. Never had I had to beg anybody to jack me off. My cock was of the gargantuan size and any guy in his right mind was only too happy to suck me off, jack me off, whatever the fuck it took to get me in motion. Shit man, I felt as if I could fly right out of my damned socks as I lay there having my tits sucked.

"MMMMM, that sure does feel good and all that you guys," I crooned. "Sure does beat having Master Jeff paddling them and mashing them down."

"Heh, if I know Master Jeff he paddled Trevor's tits down and had his slave boy Chris suck them right up again," Alex said tauntingly and quickly slurped one of my nipples back into his mouth, working it with his lips, tongue and teeth.

"H-how many of our buddies are up there at your party guys?" I asked, for lack of anything else to say at the moment.

"Oh, about fifteen to twenty guys are here," Ronald replied and swirled his tongue around and around my very erect nipple that he was working on.

My cock twitched back and forth in its massive steely hardness, pointing straight up at the ceiling, filled to the brim with piss.

"G-guys please, please, I really need to piss like a madman," I stammered pleadingly.

Alex and Ronald stopped slurping and teasing my nipples. A

few seconds later Alex was holding my cock straight out with the tip of an empty mineral water bottle over it as I pissed long, hard and white into said bottle. Ronald was holding my bulging balls in his hand, gently squeezing them every few seconds or so.

"Fuck, I get the feeling he's going to fill this entire water bottle," Alex chortled.

"Fuckers, what are you guys planning on doing with all these bottles of my piss?" I garbled angrily and the two men laughed hysterically. "Damn, I am hornier than I've ever been in all my damned life. Say Alex, how about strokin' my horse cock a few times after I'm done pissing my frothy mess into that bottle?"

"Not a chance Trevor," Alex said and simply held my manhood by the shaft, as I pissed and pissed and pissed into the water bottle. "Like we told you bud, we're saving that for after the party. And what a party that is going to be."

"Yeah, he'll be cumming as much as he's been pissing," Ronald laughed, gently massaging my bulging balls in his hand and watching as I pissed and pissed into the bottle.

When I was done pissing Alex placed the bottle on the floor along with all the others that contained my piss offerings.

"Okay Ronald, lets wipe him down a bit, make sure those straps are still good and tight and then start cooking him again," Alex said.

My two buddies wiped all the sweat off my muscular body, paying special attention to my tits, squeezing them meanly through the towels as they wiped me down. When they were done they checked to see that the straps were still holding me down and secured to the table. They didn't want me managing to slip free of them while I was all sweaty and slippery after all. When Alex undid one of the straps around my wrist I tried to yank my wrist free, but alas, I was weakened from all the heat I had endured and I just wasn't fast enough. As I was about to yank my wrist out of the confines of the strap Alex quickly pulled it tight and taut, again securing my wrist to the table.

"AAAARRRHHHHH sssssshhhhiiiittt!!!" I ranted miserably and my cock oozed massive droplets of pre cum.

Ronald quickly did the same with the strap around my other wrist and the ones over my upper and lower body.

"Yeah, he's strapped in good and fucking tight," Alex said, sounding reassured, moving down to my socked feet.

He leaned down over my feet and flicked his tongue over my

toes a few times.

"Phew, his feet sure do stink man," Alex said. "Fuck, I'm surprised none of the guys decided to steal these socks off him by now. They'll make a great souvenir for someone when this is all over."

"Yeah, like us," Ronald said and they moved to the door of the steam room.

"Okay Big guy Haynes, we have to get back upstairs to the party," Alex said to me, his hand on the control valve for the steam. "We are the hosts after all."

He turned the valve all the way up and then once again mounds upon mounds of steam were caressing me. With the empty glass from the health drink mixed with the aphrodisiac in hand Alex left the steam room with Ronald.

"Fuck, fuck," I whimpered and started sweating all over again.

Through the steam I watched as my cock twitched long and hard, pointing straight up again at the ceiling. The tip of it seemed to be yawning and more droplets of pre cum emanated from my wide sexy slit.

"OOOOOHHHH soon big guy, real soon," I whispered, trying to reassure myself that Alex and Ronald would soon let me shoot my load.

A few minutes went by and then the door to the steam room opened. I gulped hard when I saw that vulture Slave boy Chris enter with two of his sinister buddies in tow.

"I can't believe that Master Jeff let you come down here without him Chris," Lenny, a five foot seven inch tall guy with brown hair styled a-la Julius Caesar said as he came into the steam room behind Chris.

"Well Master Jeff is busy with his spanking buddies up there, exchanging notes and what have you," Chris said as they approached the table, Lenny making a bee line to my smelly feet, his drink in hand. "He won't mind if I'm gone for a few minutes. Besides, I really wanted another go at Big guy Haynes here. Check him out guys, all strapped down and totally helpless to stop us from doing whatever the fuck we want to him."

"Shit, he looks better than the buffet they're serving upstairs," Frank, a red-headed and red bearded guy of just about six feet tall said, standing beside the table.

Frank sipped his drink, squeezed one of my nipples real hard and asked me how I was doing. I replied by telling him that I would be doing a hell of a lot better if one of them would jack me the fuck off. All three of the men laughed meanly, knowing that that was the one thing they could not do for me. Everything else though was open to discussion, including, oh GAWD, the bottle of scotch that Slave boy Chris was holding in his hand.

"Okay Big fucking guy Haynes," Chris said, holding up the bottle of scotch. "Are you ready to get down and party? I felt so bad about the fact that you're missing all the fun upstairs that I thought I would bring you a drink, or a few."

"OHHHHHH," I gasped as Frank leaned down and began slathering his tongue over and over my big hairy balls. "WH-what do you have in mind you vulture?"

"Just want to get you a little tipsy you big stud," Chris replied and took the funnel from the storage area under the massage table.

"Ea-easy with my gonads you fucker," I ranted at Frank as Lenny was having a grand time squatting at the end of the table and running the tip of his tongue up and down and up and down the bottom of one of my feet.

"Five minutes guys, then we feed him the scotch," Chris said, twisting the cap off the bottle. "And he's going to get it the same way that Alex and Ronald fed him the aphrodisiac."

"OHHHHHHHH fffuuuuccccckkk, Chr-Chris, y-you wouldn't!!" I gasped, lifting my head up off the table.

"Ah, but I will," Chris said, placing a palm over my sweat sopped forehead and gently pushing my head back down, holding the bottle of scotch and the funnel in his other hand.

"*Ohhhhhhh fuck,*" I whimpered as Frank and Lenny had a grand time with my balls and feet.

Five minutes later they had the table in an upright diagonal position my feet in the air, my damned stinky asshole exposed and gaping for their perverse pleasures.

"Fuck man, look at the size of that pussy hole of his," Lenny said, sliding two sweat slicked fingers deep into my opening. "Nice and moist and tight in there too guys."

"Yeah, sure wish we can plug him a few times while we're here," Frank said and stuck three fingers inside me after Lenny had slid his out.

"AAAYYYYRRR fuckers, that ain't a damned pussy hole you're teasing," I ranted miserably and then with a sadistic looking grin on his face Slave boy Chris slid the stem of the funnel into my hole, after Frank had slid his fingers out of course.

"Are you ready to be more drunk than ever before in your life Big guy Haynes?" Chris asked me, holding up the bottle of scotch.

"Chr-Chris don't," I stammered desperately. "Alex and Ronald will get you for this man!"

I doubt that," Chris said and began slowly pouring the scotch through the funnel.

"Give it to him just a little at a time Chris," Lenny said. "Too much and he could really go flying."

Half a bottle of scotch later Chris slid the funnel out of my hole. It came out followed by a loud smelly fart.

"Whoa man, that was nasty," Chris said, laughing and waving a hand over his face.

"Y-you bastards, I-I can't even see straight n-now," I reeled in my drunken state as the table was returned to its rightful position.

The mixture of the aphrodisiac and the scotch speeding through me was driving me insane. Fuck, when were they going to let me out of the damned steam room?"

Through blurred vision and with my head spinning at what seemed like a thousand miles an hour I watched as Chris and Lenny undid the straps over my legs, leaving my upper body strapped down tight.

"WH-what are you jokers up to now?" I garbled, knowing all too well what I was in for next.

Now that they had gotten me good and sloshing drunk they were going to fulfill Frank's wish, *to plug me a few times each.* Frank, being that he had the biggest cock of the three men was going to get to go first. Chris and Lenny hoisted my legs into the air by my calves and socked ankles and spread them out good and fucking wide. I have to say that the way the fronts of my socks were sort of dangling off my toes looked real sexy from the way some of the guys had sucked at them. Looking straight up through blurred vision I took drunken note of that. My scotch-sopped hole was moist, gaping and a perfect target as Frank threw off his towel and climbed onto the table.

"OHHHHHH GAWD," I warbled drunkenly. "Pr-pretty big cock for a white boy."

"Heh, all of us Irish guys have nice sized boners Haynes," Frank said and sat with his cock pressed against the walls of my hole.

"OHHHHHHH fuccccckkk man," I panted as the guy started entering me inch by inch.

"Yeah, that's about the size of it you big stud, *fuck,*" Frank panted in a man's passion as he pressed himself up against me, his cock halfway into my hole.

He ran his hands over and over the backs of my raised and spread legs as he began thrusting like crazy inside me.

"OH yeah, fuck him Frank, fuck that stud real good," Chris chirped from the side of the table as he and Lenny watched as Frank's big Irish meat stick thrust in and out and in and out of me.

"OHHHHHH GAWD feels so fucking good and hot in there, what a great thing Alex and Ronald did in cooking this guy, he's warm inside and out," Frank panted. "I could fuck Big guy Haynes all night! Hold his legs tight you guys!"

As he fucked me Frank gave the backs of my thighs a few hard open-handed slaps each. I curled my toes back under my socks and was sweating more than profusely at that point. The need to piss had set in big and heavy again.

"OHHHHHH GOD almighty you guys, I-I'm getting close already," Frank gasped madly. "Fucking Big guy Haynes drives me batty!"

Amazingly Frank fucked me for another few minutes, making me grunt and pant like a marine before he spewed his hefty white boy load inside me.

"OHHHHH yeah, fucking A, totally fucking A you guys!!" Frank grunted wildly, holding tight to the backs of my legs as he filled my hole with his love juices.

"I get to go next," Chris said with a snide looking grin on his face. "Man oh man Big guy Haynes, your legs are going to sure be hurting by the time we get done fucking the tar out of you."

"Y-you bastard Chris," I sniveled, looking at the guy through blurred vision. "I-I still say Alex and Ronald are going to get you for making me drunk like this!"

Frank's cock slipped out of my hole after a few last thrusts. Satiated for the moment he climbed down off the table and took hold of my leg that Chris was holding up.

"Keep him spread good and fucking wide you guys," Chris said meanly, shucked off his towel and mounted the table.

"OOOHHHHHH fffuuuccckkk," I gasped as Chris' big cock entered me and sure enough my spread legs were starting to feel more than a tad sore.

"OH YEAH, thanks for warming it up in here for me Frank," Chris chortled.

Frank and Lenny stole licks and sucks on my thighs and legs as Chris fucked me and fucked me and fucked me.

"OHHHHHH man, got-got to get out of this damned steam room soon," I mumbled. "I am better than thoroughly cooked."

After Chris shot his load inside me Lenny mounted the table, but didn't need Chris and Frank to hold my legs up and spread for him. Instead the sadistic bastard pushed my legs back as far as possible and mounted me, sliding his huge meat stick into me inch by painful inch. He leered down at me and kissed and sucked my fat tits as he fucked me and fucked me and fucked me. Looking up I grinned stupidly from ear to ear at the sight of the tips of my socks hanging away from my toes.

All totaled the three men fucked me twice each, filling my hole with their thick splooge each time.

"Oh man, that was fucking enormous," Frank said, tying his towel back around his waist. "I'm going to need a cold drink when we get back upstairs."

"How about a warm drink right now?" Chris asked, holding up one of the bottles of my yellow piss.

"I uh, I don't think so Chris, I'm not too much into drinking a guy's piss," Frank said.

"If it's from a sexy stud like Big guy Haynes I'll be into it," Lenny said and took the bottle from Chris.

Lenny and Chris each took a few hearty swigs from the bottle and watching them made my hard cock twitch even more. Before leaving the steam room they strapped my legs back down to the table and I must say that it was a relief to have my poor legs stretched out again...

And so, that is how I came to be in the predicament that I am telling you about. Not all the guys from the grand opening party came down to have at me, but the ones that did sure did know how to drive me crazy that's for sure. Now, as the latest four of Alex and Ronald's friends feasted on me I wondered how much longer those guys would keep me in the steam room for. I was sure at that point that I had been in there for a lot more than just a couple of hours. The bottles of my piss placed against the wall on the floor attested to that. One of the guys stopped working me to feed me still another bottle of cool mineral water. I sipped it slowly and chills coursed through me as one of the other guys slathered my balls meanly with his tongue...

"OHHHHHH man, this guy has two of the biggest and smelliest balls I've ever had the pleasure to suck on," the guy said ecstatically. "Come on, lets all take a turn at them guys."

"AAAYYYRRRR GAWD, ea-easy with my balls you fuckers," I sputtered in my drunken state as two of the guys sucked and slurped heartily at my testicles while the other two chowed meanly on my nipples.

My balls were feeling beyond sensitive and were bulging with my juices at that point.

"S-say how about one of you jokesters giving my cock some of that sucking attention?" I asked; knowing all too well that my request would be ignored.

Beads of piss leaked from my slit and when the guys had had enough of tormenting my balls (and the heat) one of them held the tip of the newly empty mineral water bottle over my piss opening and I pissed into it. Like the last few times it seemed that I would piss and piss and piss forever. The guy held my horse cock straight out and watched in awe as my pissing seemed to just go on and on. Two of his buddies leaned to kiss me hard on the mouth as I went on pissing like crazy. When I was done the guy who had held my cock steady while I pissed took a few swigs of my fresh warm mess from the bottle.

"Well Big guy Haynes, it's time for all of us to get back to the party," the first guy said to me as all four of the guys walked toward the door of the steam room. "But don't worry; I'm sure you won't be alone all that long in here."

"Fuckers!! Damned tricksters!" I ranted and squirmed miserably under the straps as they exited the steam room, closing the door behind them.

I closed my eyes and did my best to breathe evenly. I didn't even hear the door open again because when I opened my eyes I saw Alex and Ronald standing over me, both of them now dressed in shorts, tank tops and sneakers. I must have conked out (passed out?) at some point because as I opened my eyes I realized two things. The first thing was that the steam had been turned off and the room had cooled down. The second thing I noticed was that I was no longer strapped down to the table.

"OHHHHHH man, is-is the party over?" I asked, slowly sitting up on my elbows.

"Yeah, Big guy Haynes, the party upstairs is over," Alex said. "All of our buddies have left. But *our* party is just getting started."

"I sure as hell hope that you jokers aren't planning on strapping me back down to this damned table," I said, trying to sound as threatening as possible in my weakened state. "I don't think I would be able to deal with the heat anymore."

"No, we aren't planning on doing that to you again, at least not at this time," Alex said and he and Ronald chuckled softly.

"You sure were a good sport about it all," Ronald said, taking one of my nipples between his thumb and fingers and squeezing it hard. "I mean, staying in here and being cooked and tormented all that time."

"F-fuckers didn't give me all that much of a choice did you now?" I asked in response as Ronald tweaked and squeezed my nipple, sending thrills and chills through me.

I lay back on the table and looked up at my two so called buddies, my huge horse cock again hard as a rock and pointing up at the ceiling. Alex ran a hand over my big chest and squeezed my other nipple.

"Fuck man, the heat in here really sapped my energy," I said softly, looking down at my crusty hardness. "Fuck it all man, but I sure am just about ready to shoot a WHOPPER of a fucking load."

"Not just yet Trevor," Alex said and the two men quickly grabbed my wrists, preventing me from grabbing my big throbber.

"Fuckers," I whispered as they helped me off the table, my cock throbbing and my balls aching for release between my legs.

"We had our party upstairs Big guy Haynes, now it's your turn to enjoy some festivities up there in our new gym," Alex said, looking at me with that shit-eating grin of his on his face.

I didn't do anything to stop the guy as Ronald tied a white cloth blindfold over my eyes.

"Okay, let's takes him upstairs," Ronald said, bent me over and hoisted me across his huge, broad and strong shoulders.

"Uhhhhhhhfff, thanks for the lift man," I said as we exited the steam room and slowly went up the stairs to the gym.

Ronald pressed a hand against my naked ass and slid two fingers into my sopped hole as he lugged me along. That really got a groan or two out of me let me tell you.

In the gym Ronald put me down on my socked feet and I stood there docile and blindfolded in just my damned socks with my hard horse cock sticking out nice and big and fat in front of me. Massive sized beads of pre cum oozed from my wide sexy slit and hung off the tip of my manhood. Man, was that sexy or what? Alex and Ronald each grabbed one of my wrists, stretched my arms out and slightly above me and then they were tying rope around and around my wrists.

"H-hey, what are you two jokers up to now?" I asked angrily. "Tying me the fuck up this time?"

When my stretched out arms were lashed tightly by the wrists to whatever the fuck it was they were tying me to they proceeded to do the same thing with my legs. They stretched my legs out at the ankles, toying with my socks as they did so and then began tying rope around my ankles as well. A few minutes later I was stretched out real tight and tied in a standing spread-eagled position of sorts, every fucking part of my muscular sexy black body available to the two trick players.

"Fuck it all you guys, what's the point of all this now?" I asked them miserably.

"Feeling good Big guy Haynes?" Alex asked from behind me, squeezing one of my delectable ass cheeks as he spoke. "Still feeling real fucking horny? Still aching to shoot a load or a few?"

"Fuck yeah, hell *yeah,*" I grunted through clenched teeth. "You guys know it man!!"

"I'll bet you're glad we pumped all of that Spanish fly into you eh Big guy?" Alex asked me tauntingly and placed his fingers on the knot in my blindfold.

"Yeah, got me all worked up and in a real heated lather, literally," I replied.

Chuckling, Alex took the blindfold off me. In unison six guys (Master Jeff, Slave boy Chris, Alex, Ronald, Dennis and Howard) shouted "Surprise" at me. They were standing around me, all of them looking hungrily and lustfully at my big throbbing manhood of a horse cock.

"Oh shit," I whispered and tried to manage a grin.

I took in the fact that I was securely lashed to a square metal workout device with pulleys and hooks attached to it for various types of weights and apparatuses.

"Well Big guy Haynes, you wanted to be made to shoot your load a few times right?" Alex asked me mockingly. "Well, I guarantee that before this night is over you will be better than milked dry."

I stood there feeling totally helpless, angry and horny as all six of my buddies laughed and cackled...

Fuckers, jokesters, goddamned tricksters...

ABOUT THE AUTHOR

Christopher Trevor was born in July 1963 and grew up in New York City. As soon as he was old enough to know how he began writing fiction and has been writing gay erotic/fetish stories for the past ten to twelve years at this point. He became an avid reader as well from the time he knew how and reads everything from fiction, to non-fiction to biographies of interesting and unusual people, people who have made a difference or who have paved the way for others. Christopher attributes his writing artistic inspiration to artists such as Etienne, Tom of Finland, Tagame, The Hun, and most notably Joe T, who Christopher has had the pleasure of speaking with and even meeting over the last few years. Christopher states, "Joe T encouraged me to write about my fetish because I was embarrassed about it at the time. Joe T said that when we are embarrassed about something that makes it even more enticing somehow." Christopher totally agreed and never stopped writing in this genre. Erotic writers who inspired Christopher Trevor were: Tom Shaw (author of "That Day at the Quarry), C.S. White (author of Big Sur), Larry Townsend (author of countless erotic novels), and Mason Powell (author of the classic story "The Brig.")

Christopher discovered that not only did he enjoy writing erotic tales but that after his first bondage experience he had a genuine flair for it. Writing to erotic oriented magazines about his first bondage experience truly opened the floodgates for Christopher where this style of writing is concerned. Christopher thanks the handsome and muscular "Greg" for that experience way back in time. Christopher took "Creative Writing" courses every semester during his high school years and while other friends of his stopped writing what they loved to write about as time went on Christopher never let a day go by when he didn't write something… "I feel that if I don't write every day I will die," Christopher has said many times over.

Foot fetish stories and all things related; spanking fetish, erotic shaving, muscle bondage, tickle torture, and hardcore stories are just a few of the areas of gay eroticism that Christopher enjoys writing about and inspiring in others as well. As one internet buddy said to Christopher where the black socks fetish is concerned, "Until I started talking with you I never gave a thought to my socks when I got dressed for work in the morning. Now when I pull my dress socks on every morning I get a chill up my spine."

Christopher is proud of the erotic effect he has on people…

Christopher Trevor is also the author of:

The Executive Guide to Foot Fetishism and Office Discipline
1-887895-36-1

Executive Ties That Bind
1-887895-37-X

Don't!! Stop!! That Tickles!!
1-887895-31-0

The Taming of Dominick
1-887895-45-0

Timmy and The Hong Kong Tailor
1-887895-30-2

Love, Torture and Redemption
1-887895-32-9

Timmys Ticklish Trials
978-1-887895-74-3

The Gym Instructor
978-1-887895-44-6

Milked
978-1-887895-66-8

Erotic Street Blues
978-1-887895-97-2

The Abusive Wager
978-1-887895-04-0

Look for them where you found this book or Goodboner.com.

www.ingramcontent.com/pod-product-compliance
Lightning Source LLC
Chambersburg PA
CBHW071222260626
47162CB00004B/1395